THE
DARK PLACE

Britney S. Lewis

HYPERION

Los Angeles   New York

First Edition, August 2023
10 9 8 7 6 5 4 3 2 1
FAC-004510-23166

Printed in the United States of America

This book is set in Baskerville MT Pro/Monotype.
Designed by Zareen Johnson

Library of Congress Cataloging-in-Publication Data
Names: Lewis, Britney S., author.
Title: The dark place / by Britney S. Lewis.
Description: First edition. • Los Angeles ; New York : Hyperion, 2023. •
Audience: Ages 12–18. • Audience: Grades 10–12. • Summary: Seventeen-year-old
Hylee is mysteriously sucked back in time to the worst night of her life and
must solve the mystery behind her brother Bubba's disappearance.
Identifiers: LCCN 2022037970 (print) • LCCN 2022037971 (ebook) •
ISBN 9781368077736 (hardcover) • ISBN 9781368096324 (ebk)
Subjects: CYAC: Time travel—Fiction. • Missing persons—Fiction. • African
Americans—Fiction. • High schools—Fiction. • Schools—Fiction.
Classification: LCC PZ7.1.L5125 Dar 2023 (print) • LCC
PZ7.1.L5125 (ebook) • DDC [Fic]—dc23
LC record available at https://lccn.loc.gov/2022037970
LC ebook record available at https://lccn.loc.gov/2022037971

Reinforced binding

Visit www.HyperionTeens.com

SUSTAINABLE FORESTRY INITIATIVE

Certified Sourcing

www.forests.org
SFI-01681

Logo Applies to Text Stock Only

To Grandpa, the first writer I ever met.

And to the one who has felt like you've had to
live with monsters in your past.
Tell your story.

ONE

PAST: NOVEMBER, NINE YEARS AGO

This is what I remembered.

Our house was draped in a sheet of mahogany from the dark, cold evening. Brown shingles covered two stories, and I hated the shingles. Couldn't exactly pinpoint it, just that sometimes, in the night, the house looked like it might devour every limb on our bodies and chew us into small, meaty pieces.

The tree in the front yard had thin, warping branches, and with the evening glow against the curtains, it looked like someone was reaching, stretching for the window. Bulbed knuckles and long nails. A scrape there. And maybe a whisper.

Mama had finished cooking hours ago, but the smell of warm grease stuck to the roof of my mouth while I sat in the living room, controller in hand, playing *Mortal Kombat* with my older brother, Bubba. I was eight then. He was fifteen.

I was winning, but I'd never know if it was because that random key combination I pressed with haste worked, or because Bubba was going soft on me. He'd been doing that more, and I didn't like it. I wasn't a baby. I'd be in the double digits soon.

Our older cousin Juice stretched his legs out on the couch opposite us. "I'm next," he reminded, but his eyes were on his phone while he scrolled. He'd kept saying he was up next, but Bubba and I could have gone on like that for hours and Juice wouldn't have noticed.

"Hylee!" It was a sound I refused to register, one that I'd apparently "missed three times." Mama came hurrying around the corner, her shoulder-length black hair swooshing, dark brown eyes narrowed, teeth clenched. "What did I say?"

Bubba paused the game, and I felt my mouth open, but I didn't want to go make my bed like she asked me to. If I made my bed, I'd have to *go* to bed, and I wanted to hang out with Bubba and my older cousin.

So I shrugged my shoulders. "I don't know," I lied.

Her dark painted lips folded. "Hylee Marshay . . . get up, now."

I stomped my feet, dropped the controller, and fell back onto the couch. "Ughh. I don't want to."

"Hylee," Mama said again, her voice so thin it could slice all of us in half.

Bubba helped me to my feet. "Lee, come on. You know you'll get in trouble if you act up."

"But I just want to stay and play with you and Juice."

He lowered his voice and got to my level. I could still see Mama at the corner of the living room and the hallway, a dish towel draped over her shoulder, her diamond earrings and gold chains shimmering. "Look, if you listen to Mama and make your bed, I promise . . . I'll bring the game into your room, and we can play until you get sleepy. Okay?"

I gasped. *"Really?"*

He turned to look at Mama, waiting, her arms crossed tightly, and then he lowered his voice and turned back to me. "Really." Bubba held a pinkie to the sky. "I promise," he said, and I folded my pinkie around his. Bubba never broke promises. Never, ever. But it was then when I felt like the four walls around me crept closer. And small—I felt like the smallest of creatures being sucked whole through a straw by a monster.

Mama said my name again, but her voice sounded like it was underwater. I locked my eyes on my older brother as I walked away. His brown eyes so big, like Daddy's, and hopeful. A smile, and he whispered, *"Go,"* and I went, marching past Mama in the hallway.

My bedroom was at the end of it, a small lamp on, illuminating the space. Mama flipped on the light switch, coming in behind me. "What's with the attitude, Ms. Thing?"

I huffed and plopped on my bare bed, crossing my arms and glaring at the alarm clock. Bright red characters read: 9:00 P.M. I wanted to say something but didn't. Too upset that I couldn't play with Bubba when I was winning, and too distracted by the sound in the corner of my bedroom. It was like the window was breathing these slow, shallow breaths. The blinds moving just slightly. The sound. In and out. In and out. In and out.

"Hylee?"

I snapped my head to see her, her shoe tapping into the carpet— muted but still there. I got off the bed and picked up the thin sheet with the weird edges. It always went on first. I stretched it over the blue mattress, and then I grabbed the next sheet. Took my time as I flattened it on the bed. No wrinkles as I smoothed it out with my palms.

Mama watched me crumble to the floor as I tussled with my

comforter. Pulled it here and there, trying to find where the tag was. I brought the blanket to my face, inhaled and smelled the fresh detergent. My eyes felt heavy. My fingers and toes tingled a little.

"You gotta pick up the pace," she said. "You were supposed to do this thirty minutes ago."

I rolled my eyes, my twisties moving as I engulfed the blanket in my arms. "Mama, I'm hurrying, but the blankets have to go on in order."

She made a sound like she was fed up. Her lips pursed. "When I come back, this better be done."

I tried mocking her, puckering my lips out and saying *"This better be done"* as I threw my comforter on the bed.

When the blanket was how I liked it, I tossed the pillows on, throwing one so hard it fell back off. It was 9:10 now.

I grabbed it, and then there was a bang. Like someone pounding on a door, but it wasn't mine. I paused as the sound came again, louder. I stretched my neck.

It was out *there* . . . past the hallway . . . the front door.

Daddy shouted—asked who was there—but his voice . . . something sounded wrong with it. It wobbled a little, like how mine did when I was scared.

Bang.

It wasn't a gun. It was the sound of something breaking. Wood splitting. A thud, a thud, a thud, and silence, until I heard what sounded like feet running and slipping on carpet and wood.

Bang.

Jumped to my feet, my hands balled into small fists as I hurried to my bedroom door. *That* was a gun. It was so loud and so sharp, my eardrums rumbled. Nothing but the sound of a machine flatlining. A hum. I almost didn't hear someone shout for me out there.

Out.

There.

My fingers trembled as I reached for the doorknob. Twisted it slowly, my breath heavy, my chest stretching rhythmically to my fear.

And that was it.

That was all I remembered.

TWO

PRESENT DAY: FEBRUARY

The inside of my mouth was raw from all the biting.

Torn a little, a scab probably forming.

A subtle taste of rust on the tip of my tongue.

It was the night before my first day at my new school now that I was living with Grandmommy, and the disappearing was all I could think about. A magic act, you could say. But it wasn't. I didn't mean to disappear....

I shifted in bed, half-asleep, half-awake, hearing the sound of my name over and over again in my head.

It was a sharp whisper, and the more I listened to it, the more I didn't know if the voice was mine. It was almost like the day of the incident, nine years ago, stuck, unsure of what was to come.

My silk scarf made a sound on my cotton pillowcase as I turned. Turned again. Moonlight shining in between the slats of the white blinds. I held my phone, waiting for Lucia to text me back, even though it was late.

I knew she'd be up—she was a night owl, always awake when I was asleep, and tonight, I didn't want to sleep. I was afraid of slipping, of falling into whatever that *other* place was that I'd fallen into last Sunday. The thing was, I didn't know what happened last week. One moment I was at the family cookout and the next? Gone. I vanished into thin air, then reappeared as if nothing had happened. But it *had*.

Watching me vanish must have changed something for my parents. The look in Daddy's hazel eyes, the way they glossed over—it told me things were different. Grandmommy wore the same look, with the same eyes, when she picked me up from my parents' rental this morning. She hugged me, her bones stiff like she was frozen, her stare cutting right through me as if I weren't there at all. Then she helped me carry my things to her car. We loaded the trunk and the backseat.

Once we were on the road, she looked over at me, twisting her lips in the same way that I did, but she looked repulsed, like she'd spit me out if she had to taste any of my sour thoughts. Like I was not safe or palatable. I was unpredictable, and I knew that when my family looked at me now, they saw something different.

But it was the waiting that was unbearable.

The waiting that made me want to open the car door at the traffic light and walk down the street while I waited for Grandmommy to ask what happened. She hadn't been at the cookout, so she didn't witness it like Mama, Daddy, or my friend Lucia had. After, my parents were stammering and yelling, *"What the fuck just happened?"* While Lucia looked catatonic and whispered, "What?" under her breath repeatedly.

But not Grandmommy. Not as I sat next to her in her car, and as she pressed on the gas, all she could get out was "Are you sure you're okay?" With that look on her face, *s p i t t i n g . . . me . . . o u t.*

I said, "Yeah," and I knew that *she* knew it was a lie. But it was all I had, and that would have to be enough, because I didn't understand what happened, and I felt like I was losing my sanity. I had to have imagined it, disappearing, but it felt so real.

I mean, it was real.

As I thought it over, I picked up my phone again and held it to my face, trying to will a text message to appear. Like everyone else, Lucia had been acting weird since I disappeared. I get it, it was strange, but for her to ignore me completely...that didn't seem right. She was my friend, and I needed her.

I grumbled, kicked away my sheets. Texted Lucia again.

> Hey
>
> Did u get my last txt???
>
> Could really use a friend rn

I locked my phone right after I sent it because I felt sorry for myself and embarrassed. Desperate, even. This was text number four since I vanished, and still, nothing.

Got up then, turned on my lamp, and dug through my book bag, pulling out my drawing pad and my pencil case. Placed everything on the little desk Grandmommy had left in this room—pencils to the right of the pad, erasers to the left. The desk itself sat by the window, and I pulled the blinds up to see what the night looked like here.

It wasn't the same as it was in the city. See, Grandmommy lived on this cul-de-sac in a two-story home, and her backyard was on the edge of the street. The people here *actually* had those white picket fences. It was funny because I'd only ever heard them mentioned in songs, but there they were. Very, very white. Very, very real.

Grandmommy had worked her way up to head of accounting

for the city, and now she lived in Brindleton Bay, a new suburb in Lee's Summit, Missouri, about thirty minutes away from Kansas City, Kansas. Apparently, I lived here, too. Semipermanently, anyway.

The night in Brindleton Bay was different because it was darker—not enough light from buildings or houses, no glowing neon signs, no phones shining from people who wandered in the evening. Just darkness. And quiet.

I could see every twinkle in the midnight sky, the moon's face looking directly at me. Deer, and maybe a car or two. A raccoon, a possum. Country shit.

Before I drew, I crept out of my bedroom and down the staircase to the kitchen in search of the tea Grandmommy made earlier. It was probably cold now, in the fridge.

The floor creaked every third step, and I used the flashlight on my phone to light up my path. A turn, and to my surprise, Grandmommy was there, sitting at the island with a cup of tea in her hands.

"Well, shit." Her eyes were wide, her mouth snapping shut as she held her hand to her chest. Her long brown hair was braided back, a scarf tied across her edges. She had just turned sixty and only had a few strands of gray hair. "You 'bout scared the living out of me. You've been so quiet tonight, I forgot you were here."

Normally, I would have laughed at Grandmommy—I would

have poked fun at how frazzled she looked, but I couldn't tonight. That part of my brain was turned off because all I could think about was what happened when I disappeared and then after.

I was ripped right away from the couch, and suddenly I was on my feet, at our old family house, in the night. It was brown and waiting. So much bigger than I remembered it. Haunting. There was that flickering light on the back porch, the stillness, and that girl. The way her mouth was, how she didn't have any eyes, and the familiarity and terror I felt when she touched me: cold and afraid, but also like I was missing something.

"Sorry, Grandmommy," I said, trying to shush the memories away. "I just wanted some tea. Couldn't sleep much. It's too quiet here."

She smacked her lips. "I know, I know. But you'll get used to it," she said, and it sounded like something she repeated to herself until it was true. A manifestation. I wondered how long it had taken for her to adjust to the suburbs. She'd been out here for six years now, but it didn't feel like it.

A kettle was set on the stove, the water still warm. I grabbed a tea bag and poured the water into an old white mug before dunking the bag in.

"Why are you up, anyway? Are you nervous about your new school tomorrow?" Grandmommy asked.

I shrugged as I took a sip. "Kind of. Not sure what the people are like here."

She nodded, her hands clasping her mug, and inside me, I felt a tugging, like little fingers were pulling down on my ribs, and since Grandmommy hadn't asked yet, I wondered how she felt about the whole thing.

"Grandmommy, do you think what happened to me was real?"

She furrowed her brow, held her mug tighter—I could see the tips of her fingers turning a shade of red—and she took a sip. "Do I . . . think it was real?" she said, and the way she said it, how it was all drawn out, made me feel like she was reminding herself that I'd spoken. Her eyes shifted around the dimly lit kitchen. The darkness around her seeming darker than before. "Was it *real*?" she said again. "Why would you ask that?"

My eyes welled, and I felt the warmness flooding my body. I wasn't even sad, I was angry. Because of *that*. Because she couldn't answer the question. And while earlier I'd nibbled at the thought that it was okay she didn't bring it up, that maybe it brought peace, I knew now that it wasn't, and her silence on the issue made me feel so small and so weak, like I'd been tucked away and every movement I made was invisible.

And it was odd of her. Grandmommy always had something to say. Always inserted her opinion even when it wasn't wanted.

"Because we haven't talked about it," I said, and I would not let my voice break. I would not. I would be strong. I would say what I meant, and only—only as a last resort would I lie. "And it was strange, and everyone else freaked out because how could this happen, but you haven't... I mean, you haven't said anything, and I don't know why. And I'm afraid that if we don't talk about it, we'll forget. It'd be like when our house got broken into all over again. Like when Bubba—"

Grandmommy's deep sigh cut me off, and she scooted her chair away from the island, that sound so harsh against reality that I twitched as she got up to walk toward me. Her arms open, her plaid pajamas swishing a hard cotton sound before they welcomed me in. The voice in my head was back, growing louder: *Hylee*.

Pressed my face against Grandmommy's chest, my cheek smashing, and the smell of her chamomile tea wafted around me. I wondered how many times Grandmommy had had to comfort Daddy like this. It was only ever the two of them.

When she let me go, her hazel eyes looked crooked. Why was that? "Here's what I know, Hylee: We don't *really* know what happened Sunday. But just... leave it alone."

I wanted to crawl out of my skin. What a suggestion. "What if I don't want to leave it alone? What if I can't? What if it happens again? Then what?" I crossed my arms, pressed my back against the oven handle.

Grandmommy's jaw shifted, a deviance trickling around her irises. A tic in her face, and she stared. A look that sent me back to that *other* place, but only for a moment. Only long enough to make believe that Grandmommy's mouth was vined and twisted. The skin around her eyes gluing together now, eyes gone. Her face wrinkling like a raisin.

I almost dropped the mug, and I gasped, used my other hand to grab hold of the oven handle. I wanted to count to make it go away. I needed to count.

One.

"Go to bed, Hylee," Grandmommy said, her mouth not moving, dark shadows rising around her like smoke with tentacles.

Two.

She came closer, patted my shoulder, and I almost sank. "It'll all be fine in the morning."

Three.

I blinked, and she was herself again. My breathing eased a little, but I still felt uncomfortable. Did that really happen?

"But, *Grandmommy.*" My voice was only a whisper. If I spoke too loud, would the darkness come back?

"Good night," she said, and she walked past me, leaving the kitchen. I waited for her to come back, maybe say more, but then her bedroom door closed, and my shoulders dropped.

That was it.

The kitchen seemed eerie now that she was gone, and a rush of fear pressed into my gut. What *was* that?

I set my mug in the sink and rushed up the staircase as if someone was following behind me—step for step, right on my heels.

No one was there when I closed my bedroom door. *Even if I thought I heard something.*

I exhaled, returned to the desk, checked my phone. Still no texts. I was pissed because I was confused and alone. I didn't get why Grandmommy didn't want to talk this through with me, or why Lucia was avoiding me. I needed someone, anyone, to listen to me.

She probably thinks you're weird.

Shut up, I told my thoughts. *Just shut up.* And I sat down, took another breath, my eyes blurring. I turned on a lo-fi playlist, grabbed a soft charcoal pencil, flipped open a new page in my drawing pad. I sniffled as my eyes leaked. *Fuck. Fuck. Fuck.*

Pressed pencil to paper and drew. The act of drawing would clear my mind, bring clarity. It always had. I kept drawing until the lines on the page turned into hands. They were the hands I saw in my head the night our family home was broken into, when I was in the tub, before the officer found me. I had different versions of them, filling notebook after notebook, and I could draw them with my eyes closed if I needed to. I knew these hands better than I knew myself. But tonight, I drew them with trepidation because after I disappeared, I saw a different version of these hands in my head.

And I hoped that drawing them might help me understand them better.

THREE

PAST: FEBRUARY, TWO WEEKS AGO—
THE DISAPPEARANCE

At first, I was there.

At Mama and Daddy's new rental, which I despised.

I didn't like the smell—it was this old, milky thing that lingered—but I guessed it was better than the apartment complexes we'd been moving in and out of since I was nine. Nothing would ever really feel like home—not like the one I grew up in. The one where Bubba and I were twisted pinkies, always promising. Because even if everything in life was scientifically proven to end one day, our words were always forever.

It was the day before my seventeenth birthday, a Sunday, and Mama and Daddy wanted to have a small cookout.

The adults were on the back porch because Mama said even though I was turning seventeen, I still wasn't old enough to be in "grown folks' bidness." Which really meant they didn't want to teach me to play spades—a mistake on their part because should I decide to go off to college and return, my family would cause absolute havoc upon the realization that I didn't know how to play.

"You really let them white folks get to you, huh?" an uncle would say. Or, "Dang, Hylee, how you don't know how to play? You're Black!"

Yet none of that would be a surprise. They say all those things anyway.

Whatever.

Anyway, I was glad that Lucia had arrived because my cousins weren't here, and I could always count on her for a good time. Lucia and I had been besties since sixth grade when we were plopped in the same art class and assigned to sit next to each other.

Now we were on the couch in the living room, right across from the incense that was almost burned down to the end.

She was cackling over some video she'd found of a cat wailing as it tried to jump from one ledge to the other. It was the kind of funny where you laughed so hard you cried, and then you started sniffling because you were crying, and I figured I could use a laugh like that, but my stomach felt weird, uneasy. Maybe it was from how fast I'd eaten the baked beans and deviled eggs.

I stood up after but had to immediately sit back down. Felt like my head was on a Tilt-a-Whirl, and the bass from the music felt much louder than before—it blurred my vision—and I could feel it. I could *feel* the sound waves pushing through my ears. A migraine coming on, probably. It had to be.

I remember I couldn't breathe too well, a bubble of air trapped in my throat.

I remember Lucia's small voice asking if I was okay, but she felt so far away from me.

I remember one of Mama's beauty shop friends tapping my shoulder. She must have come out of nowhere, but I could still smell the oil sheen in her hair.

I remember Daddy's voice growing louder over the music, shouting my name like it would avert the coming, like it would avert what was about to happen next. He—he must have come from nowhere, too.

I thought I'd tilt my head back, to rest it, just for a second, just for a moment, but in that instant, I felt myself sink.

The sofa engulfed me like dough rising around fingers.

And then.

And then there was no light.

My joints felt disconnected from my body, my limbs gooey. All I could hear was my breath at first, the way it accelerated.

It was fire, electricity, and *something* more—much, much more.

When I ended up—*where* I ended up—it was night, and the stillness was so frigid, I felt my cheeks crack from the cold. I was in the backyard of my childhood home. I knew I was because I recognized that big tree there, the way it shifted and bent over the wooden gazebo, the way the arms stretched out nakedly, like it wanted to scoop me up.

And the light, on the back porch, the way it was greenish and flickering. Always flickering. And the edge of the driveway, where I stood, the way it crumbled at the end, the way it ruined me and Bubba's waterslide.

How did I get here?

The night was too quiet to feel real. No wind. No crickets. Not even a car passing by. I pressed my arms against my abdomen. Chills skittering like small bugs across my brown skin, down my spine. I could hear my breath leaving my body, jagged, a light puff filling the air.

Took a step forward, up the driveway, and the porch light stopped flickering. On cue, almost, like it was waiting for me.

To the right of the driveway, in a patch of dead grass, something shiny.

I thought I should probably leave it alone. It was dark, and I didn't know where the hell I was, but it looked familiar.

I walked over to grab it, and when I pinched it between my fingers, I knew immediately. It was Bubba's coin. He always had it on him; I hadn't seen it in years. On both sides it had a skull and the words *memento mori* around the curvature.

Sirens then, the sound screeching. I pocketed the coin and ran back to the driveway. The flashing of red and blue lights bleeding into the darkness. Familiarity screaming at me. Footsteps slapping against pavement. A little Black girl running toward me from the other end of the driveway.

Running.

The ballies on the ends of her plaits clacking together. Closer, she got closer. And I could see now—I could see how her mouth twisted in the same way that vines twisted up the sides of the house. Her lips were stitched together, and the smallest, tiniest flowers budded on the edges of where her smile ended. There was skin covering where her eyes should have been. No eyelashes or anything—all of it gone.

And she would not stop coming for me.

The closer she got, the more I felt like I knew her, but I couldn't move. It felt like I couldn't breathe. My organs were filled with terror, my face numb.

Someone help me. Help me. Help!

And this had to be a dream. It had to be. Then she touched me, and I screamed, the sound ripping through my body, filling the night like the sirens. Then another voice came from somewhere, the sound of my name.

Hylee.

I was pulled into darkness again. Gone. Then a thud.

"Ow," I grumbled, my forehead bouncing back against something hard. When I opened my eyes, I could see through blurry lenses that I was back at Mama and Daddy's rental, lying on the front porch, beneath the porch light. I had been in the living room before, sitting on the couch. How— What was happening?

I lifted my head to see them, and the dizziness was back. Mama, Daddy, Lucia, and Sherie—they were all there, all wearing the same face. They looked as terrified as I had been, and confused. Their eyebrows twisted into scowls; their mouths hung low.

Was all of that real? I rolled onto my back, seeing my breath in the evening air, and when I did, I reached into my pocket, feeling the edge of cold, smooth metal. *Memento mori.* Bubba's coin.

And I knew then, I knew that it wasn't a dream. And then I threw up on the porch as reality punched me in the gut.

I had been sucked into some weird dimension.

I had been taken back to the place I hadn't been in nine years.

Not since the incident.

FOUR

PRESENT DAY: FEBRUARY

My alarm was so loud, I wanted to scream.

I grabbed for it aimlessly, turning the stupid thing off.

If only five more minutes could be stretched into eternity. Then I wouldn't have to drag myself to this new school and plod through another day wondering why I didn't have the power to make anyone or anything stay.

Moving in with Grandmommy wasn't by choice. I loved my art teacher back home. Loved my art friends (hated math and the remedial math class they made me take because I didn't understand math), but I had to live with Grandmommy because Mama and Daddy didn't know what to do with me after my sudden disappearance (and reappearance).

Yesterday, they could barely look at me as I packed my last bag. Could barely give me hugs without wondering what I'd do next. And I knew they were scared. I could tell by the way they shook a little, by the way their words were laced with sadness. "It's..." they'd start. But they never finished their sentences, too tongue-tied to let me in on their thoughts.

I understood as much as I could.

They didn't want to lose me.... They didn't want to lose another kid. Mama and Daddy opened my bedroom door and stood half in the threshold, half in the hallway as their only daughter packed her bags.

Once the door was open, Daddy's eyes were the first thing I saw. Wide, glistening. Mama pressed against him with red rims.

"You know we love you, right?" he said, but clearly love wasn't enough of a reason to keep them from kicking me out because, again, there I was, packing my last bag.

And now here I was, in this new room with beige-painted walls, trim, and crown molding. Different from the speckled, peeling stuff at Mama and Daddy's rental. No bars on the windows. No flooded basement. No lingering guests.

I felt myself drifting. Sleep always came so easy in the morning, and the dreams rushed back in like a levee had broken. The images came blurry at first, the vibrant green ivy growing up the side of my childhood home, ripping through the brown shingles. The air cold, but wet like rain had just fallen. The wind pushing through the leaves, the rustling, the smell of dying.

And I could see those hands again. Stretching toward me. Almost so close.

"Hylee."

I popped up, a thudding against my throat. It was Grandmommy in the doorway, but her voice sounded strange from here, muffled almost. Her blown-out hair was twisted into an updo, and she had on a maroon-colored blouse and dark jeans.

"Don't you turn that alarm off again," she said. "You can't be late on your first day of school. Bus will be here in thirty." She walked away after she said it, leaving the door ajar.

I groaned, grabbed my phone, and slipped under the blankets to check my notifications. There were six new texts from Lucia.

Happy first day at your new school!!!

Sry!!!!

Maybe we can talk about what happened last week some other time???

Come w me to this house party in ur neighborhood

It's this weekend

Don't ask me how I know, but u should go

We can get ready together

Two thoughts.

One. Finally. I'd been nervous she wasn't going to text me back. Out of everyone who saw me disappear last Sunday, she seemed the most terrified. She didn't look me in the eye when I came back. My parents helped me off the porch, got me inside, and Lucia seemed struck by something. People passed her by, and she stood still, her Nikes pressing into the carpet until she came undone. She left expeditiously, muttering something before she shouted "Bye." Our texts hadn't been the same since.

And two. It bugged me that Lucia didn't want to talk about it. Shit. We used to talk about everything: Bubba, first crushes, making it big someday. We were like blood sisters, and now this—it made me feel like a burden, but I needed her. I needed someone in my corner.

I hated thinking it, but we were growing apart.

It wasn't all of a sudden. It wasn't because I moved or even because I'd disappeared (though, honestly, I was sure that was a big reason). It was a cluster of different things mashing together.

She was in the KC Scholars program. Her friend group changed. We started hanging out with different people. She didn't come to any of my galleries at school. And probably the biggest reason of them all: I used to lie a lot when we were younger.

Sometimes I still did.

Eventually, she caught on because how could anyone keep a lie floating with paperweights? My stories were always lavish and changing. One week my family and I were going on adventures to Disneyland. The next week we were swimming at the Lake of the Ozarks.

There was more, too. I'd borrow clothes I liked from Lucia, but I never returned them because I knew I wouldn't get anything like it from my parents. Even when she asked for them back, I'd pretend like I'd return them, then just didn't.

I'd mold myself to like all the things that she did, and I'd overstay my welcome, spending a week at her house during the summer all because I wanted her to think I was cool. All because I was afraid that if she didn't like me, I'd have no one.

Could lying build an honest friendship? Maybe microscopically.

Even if I knew it was wrong—*it was*—I didn't think it constituted the right to say I didn't deserve love or friendship.

Because we lie and we die, and in the end, we are forgotten. It's all one and the same.

Lucia and I were crumbling. Had been for a while. We were sawdust at this point, but sawdust was still *something*. All I needed was a fleck to hold on to. But this new thing that happened to me was an inevitable tug; we were a small slit in a predestined grain line.

> Thx. Not looking forward to it, tbh
>
> I'll let you know if it turns into the whole Get Out situation
>
> But is everything ok with you?
>
> You've been super MIA
>
> And how's abuelita??? I feel like I haven't heard any updates
>
> What party? ꜱꜱ
>
> I'm down to go, but I feel like I should be cautious....

Lucia's little typing bubble popped up, but then it went away. I waited a few seconds more, hoping, but no messages came.

So I rolled out of bed, shuffled through my room and bags until I found a pair of jeans and a Mandalorian graphic T-shirt.

I refreshed my curls, and when I got downstairs, Grandmommy threw a granola bar at me. She smiled, and I contemplated bringing up the conversation from last night. Maybe she was just grumpy, and that was why she'd responded the way she had, but...I just couldn't ignore what was happening to me.

As I grabbed my jean jacket, she gave me a look that seemed so off-putting. Her head cocked to the side, and she looked dazed, a little lost.

Then she snapped out of it, said good-bye, and was gone.

I would have said bye back, but then I heard my bedroom door creak open. It was up the stairs, and since it was only the two of us, it frightened me. Then a shadow with jagged edges spilled into a corner, and I rushed out the front door as fast as possible. If I pretended I couldn't see it, I could get through the school day.

The crisp morning carried fog in the air, and it smelled of wet grass. The trees were still naked, and I longed for the day when small tufts of green poked their way through openings. Soon. But not soon enough.

The bus stop was on the end of this street, across from the cul-de-sac. I knew there were other teens in the neighborhood. I'd seen them in the past when I'd come up to visit Grandmommy. They'd bike through in herds, or linger on the benches, laughing so loud it'd echo against the identical houses.

No one else stood at the stop with me today. The stillness of it, the way the wind silenced itself and the birds refused to sing, made me feel like I'd been taken back to that place. The dark place. And I was terrified that meant I might go again. I did not want to go. But I didn't have a choice—did I?

When it happened a week ago, it was both sudden and not sudden. It whooshed over me incrementally, and all at once like rain.

It hadn't happened since then, but there was no guarantee that it wouldn't happen again.

Then, with a low sharp squeal and humming engine, the yellow bus pulled to the top of the hill. I climbed on quickly, still feeling like something lingered too close behind me. There was an empty seat at the back, and I slid into the cool gray seat, hugging my backpack close to my chest as I looked out the window.

We left Brindleton Bay, entering another subdivision behind it, and after a few more stops, we headed toward a back road, surrounded by tall, leaning trees and overgrown patches of land. No people here. Just brown and green grass that ran into naked forests. A small wooden outhouse with a crescent moon carved at the top of it. The wood separating, half of it settled farther in the ground. Must have been there for years before any of this other stuff was.

But deep in the forest, standing beside a bare tree, I saw a girl.

Brown skin and a sinking where her eyes should be. My back stiffened, and I gulped when I looked around. The person opposite me was sound asleep, body leaning against the window. Someone in the seat ahead had headphones on and laughed while scrolling on their phone. My feet tingled and my stomach turned. I closed my eyes.

After ten minutes, I relaxed again. We drove by a pasture with a herd of cows, and in front of that was Lee's Summit West High School. It was exactly how I remembered it the day we registered for classes last week. This long, two-story, U-shaped brick building with a front that stretched into a point like a ship.

And in front of the school: cows. Freaking cows.

Never in my seventeen years had I witnessed farm animals in front of a school building. They didn't do that in Wyandotte County. My old school, Schlagle, was right next to apartments, neighborhoods, a church, a gas station, and even a few stores. But never cows that mooed and stared and chewed judgingly.

I see you.

I stepped off the bus onto a sidewalk and followed a group of kids inside the building. The light stretched into the school like a greenhouse, and before me was an extended glass hallway that led to the center of the high school, to the cafeteria. To the left and to the right of that were big winding halls that wrapped around the school for what felt like miles.

I gulped, my fingers pressing into the palms of my hands. What if I disappeared here, surrounded by all these people I didn't know? What then?

Since it was my first day, I was supposed to stop in the front office before classes began. It smelled like fresh paint and papers, and behind the desk was a woman on the phone. Her head was down, and she nodded while she wrote something on a sticky note.

"Hi. Are you Hylee?" a voice asked. I didn't see her at first; she stood from a bench that was tucked off to the side. She was white and looked about my age. She had dark blond hair that was cut to her jawline and pushed behind her ears. She wore these big teardrop earrings, baggy pants, and a loose cream sweater.

I nodded, and she approached me to shake my hand. "I'm Sarah. I'm one of the student ambassadors here. I've been assigned to give you a tour today."

"Oh, hi. Nice to meet you," I said, following her out. Sarah smelled of an expensive perfume, and the way she dressed wasn't like anything I was used to back in the city. It wasn't that she dressed bad, per se, it was just that she dressed like she had money. I didn't know how I knew that. It was a guess.

Sarah was taller than me, but most people were, and in one of her hands she held a printed piece of paper. From a side glance I could tell it was my class schedule. I had a copy of it on my phone.

"Are you coming from a different state?" she asked once we got down one of the cinder-block hallways. Students lingered in corners and grooves. Some of them huddled in groups outside of classrooms, waiting for class to start. Others leaned against lockers, looking at their phones. Low chatter and mumbles spiraled around me. Two students sat at a table with a cloth that read *Future Farmers of America.*

Farmers.

And yes, okay. I knew I was from Kansas. Laugh or whatever makes you feel better, but I didn't know there were teens who joined groups to be farmers. No dig on farmers. I just didn't know anyone who wanted to be one.

"Technically, yes, but it's just Kansas City."

"Oh, no way. I have family that live downtown."

"I'm from the Kansas side," I said because there was a big difference between the two.

"So, what, did your family move up here? Parents change jobs?"

My parents had been doing the same thing my whole life. Daddy worked in some factory (off and on). Mama did hair. I didn't think they planned on changing anything anytime soon. My theory was that they thought if they never changed, somehow that stillness would bring Bubba back.

"Uh, no. Not that. We just decided that living with my grandmother was the best option for me."

Her eyes squinted a little when we got to the end of the hallway to the stairway. A look someone gave when they were curious, but she didn't press. I wondered what she thought.

"What about you? Have you always been here?"

Her shoulders slouched. "*Always* is an understatement. I feel like I've been here for an eternity."

I laughed.

"I can't wait to get out, though. I'm gonna reinvent myself." She almost strutted down the hall when she said it, her hair bouncing.

"And do what?"

"Literally anything else. I will clean toilets in New York if it means I can get away from this Podunk."

"I ain't cleaning toilets for no one, but I'll certainly join you."

She smiled and dropped her voice. "At least you have limits, because I totally don't." She laughed, hummed, and then said, "Ugh, that's probably too much. We just met. But anyway, we'd be two peas in a pod. I'll be the toilet cleaner, and you'll be the—"

"The artist." I smiled; my chin tipped toward her as my curls fell a little.

Sarah purred, and I furrowed my brow. "Honey, you're an artist? What's your specialty? What do you love? I'm a graphic designer."

"I want to be an illustrator."

A high-pitched sound came from her, and then she wrapped an arm around me, her vanilla smell like a piranha nipping at my nose. "We're gonna be the best of friends!"

I recoiled a little, and she let go quickly.

"Gah. Sorry. Personal boundaries."

"Yeah, personal boundaries are great," I said, but I smiled at her because I'd forgotten how it felt to just *be*.

Sarah explained how classes worked. How, instead of there being a block schedule, the classes were only about an hour long, and we had all our classes every day. A period schedule was what it was called.

She showed me where my locker was, and then she took me to each class. We figured out we both had pottery together, which we gleamed about, and she said she'd save me a seat.

Sarah took me to the cafeteria, the atrium, the library, and the study rooms. She showed me the elevator, the vending machines, and secret hideouts. This place felt like a fairy-tale palace compared to my old school. I didn't think worlds like this could exist for me, but then again, I didn't think disappearing and reappearing was possible, either.

My first class was on the second floor in room 221. It was English with a Black woman named Mrs. Miller.

Like the movies, we read Shakespeare's *Twelfth Night*, something I hadn't studied at my last school, at least not yet. I'd left before we had a chance to get to it.

Even with the book open in front of me, I was too distracted by the people here. The way they looked, the way they dressed. How they talked and pronounced words. Their hair—long and straight. Or short or buzzed. Some curls here and there, but not many kinks. Not many coils.

The only thing I caught from *Twelfth Night* was this:

Journeys end in lovers meeting.

FIVE

No one in my family talked about the night Bubba disappeared.

It was so frustrating, because how could you just forget some-one you loved so much? How could you put their name in a box and then hide that box from everyone in the world? They were treating him like a coffin. He was gone, but we didn't know if he was dead.

I imagined that night haunted them in their core, deep and dark and black. Fallen so far down that hole, not even light could reach them.

And I envied Mama and Daddy because at least they remembered.

My memories of that night had been cut off. There was so much I didn't know—so much I couldn't piece together. I was eight when it happened, and there were plenty of memories I could pull from a hat and tell you about, but not this one. Not completely. Google said it was due to PTSD, but it felt like something else.

What I remembered was bits and pieces of *before* and *after*.

After the house was broken into, I was tucked away in the bathroom on the first floor of the house. The bathroom was right off the hallway, and past the hallway was the living room. The living room was where I'd seen Bubba last. He was with Juice. They were playing a game without me.

I don't know how I got in the bathroom, or how long I was there, just that I sat in the tub, my heart racing, my knees pulled to my chest as I swallowed the air in big gulps, counting to three. The counting would scare the monsters away.

I kept thinking I heard my name—like someone had been shouting it at me.

Hylee, Hylee, HYLEE.

And then the bathroom door was kicked in, and I was met with a bright blinding light. Behind that light was a police officer.

Even if I tried, I couldn't remember his face—just his badge and how it glistened behind the flashlight he held, and how he scooped me out of the tub and held my hand as we walked out of the house to safety.

I remember the blood in the living room and then those red and blue lights from the cop cars and the ambulance outside.

When they delivered me to Mama, she wasn't herself.

Beautiful black hair disheveled now. An earring missing, her clothes smudged with dark marks and a splash of mahogany. I wrapped my arms around her, squeezing until I felt her ribs expand.

She tried to speak to the officers, but every word she said was gibberish. I watched her confusion when she noticed it kept happening. I heard her tongue click...click...leading to nothing. They said she was in shock.

Daddy appeared. His legs buckled beneath him. Falling and getting up as he ran. A dark red smeared his jeans, and his light brown face looked swollen. He kept saying Bubba's name.

"He was in there!" he said, and I watched the spit fly from his mouth. "We need to look everywhere!" He shouted it to the officers and the firemen. They tried to get to him, tend to his wound, but Daddy wouldn't let it be.

He took off to get back inside the house, and they tackled him to the ground. Muffled cries and shouts into the stiff November grass. He yelled for someone to hear him as they brought out a stretcher from inside the house. A fitted white sheet pressed over a person.

A person was in there.

A person was in there, no longer living.

Who? Was that Bubba?

I almost thought it was, but then another officer appeared. "Ma'am, your son, where is he? When did you see him last?" he asked.

I imagined she tried to tell them that he was here. Moments ago, he was here.

The police officer wrote something down. Spoke codes into his walkie.

I found out later that the person on the stretcher was Juice.

The police officers, they said they'd look for my brother, but they didn't know what to promise after seeing the blood. Since there had already been one body, it was possible another was nearby. Still, they weren't sure if he'd been taken for some kind of ransom, or if he'd run away to safety, but they said they'd look.

And that's it, that's all I remember. I was in the tub, and then I was out of the house, and Bubba was forever gone.

They never found a body to prove he was dead, and after years and years, the case was eventually considered "cold." No one was looking for my brother anymore. After a while, not even me.

But now, after being sucked back to that house and seeing that coin, I couldn't stop thinking about it.

SIX

PRESENT DAY: FEBRUARY

On the way to my last period, I heard feet running behind me.

It wasn't like the students walking in the hall, all around, their shoes slapping against the carpet like a muted drum. It was a pitter-patter—like the way light raindrops would hit against the panel on the back porch of Mama and Daddy's rental. And it matched my pace. Left, right, left, right.

I paused where I was, feeling my chest rise and the brownish-blond hair on my arms prickled. The mimicking footsteps stopped when I did. A stench of tangerine and rotting trash dug into my nostrils, and it took some girl shouting, "Get the fuck out the way, Princess Tiana," for me to find the courage to look behind me.

When I turned, there was nothing but an ocean of kids rushing past to their next class. Normalcy, beating hearts, and blank faces.

They swept past me quickly, the foul smell dissipating, but there was a dark haze that lingered in the corners.

One kid was all, "Cool shirt," and the rest walked by me like I didn't exist.

But then I felt sick, my stomach knuckling. The tips of my fingers tingled like I'd held my phone for too long. A queasiness that was so intense, I ran to the bathroom, bumping into people on the way in.

I held myself up in the stall, my palms pressed to the cold dividers as I lurched over the toilet. My bangs brushed my eyebrows, and my spine tremored until the room spun.

I was here. I was here. I was *here.*

Then I was gone.

A blink, and I was still lurched over a toilet, but the room was dark now.

I heard something flutter—something similar to the sound of paper-thin wings.

My gaze panned upward, and my neck felt heavy. I stared at a cabinet above the toilet. It looked burned, and through a crack, I could see something slither inside.

Then I heard a stuttered sniffle. It reminded me of a stiff staccato; all that inhaling had to lead up to tears. And then it did. Whatever was over there, started to cry.

I was too afraid to look, so I slowly let my gaze trail to the left, realizing that I was *there*. At my childhood home. In the bathroom, except this bathroom was wrong. It was calamitous, and the tiles were broken, some missing, revealing darker holes in the wall—they were so deep they could lead anywhere.

The cries came louder. The soiled tub was filled with dirt and things that crawled. In the center of the tub, a girl—

Bang.

To my right, the door was kicked in, and I screamed and screamed and screamed, covering my ears, clamping my eyes shut, until I felt a dissonance, the sound of air whirring above me.

"Are you okay?!" someone yelled.

And I stopped.

Through misty eyes I saw that I was back at the high school. In the stall. Snot running down my chin, and someone on the other side asking me if I was okay again.

I snapped off a wad of toilet paper, hid my face, and ran out of the bathroom.

Down the hall. To the glass door. Into the cold sun. No one stopped me. There was only one class left, so I skipped out on school and walked until I got to Grandmommy's. My nose cold. My arms gripping my sides.

When I got to my room, I felt something in my back pocket.

I pulled it out, it was the coin. Bubba's coin.

I dropped it, and it bounced on the carpet. I couldn't believe I had it. I'd forgotten about it, but these were the jeans I'd been wearing at the cookout, and I wondered... if I could bring the coin back with me, what else could I bring back with me?

SEVEN

After the incident at school, I hid beneath my blankets, praying and flipping the coin in my hand. I didn't pray often, or much. My family was holiday churchgoers. My maternal grandmother scolded us for that. *Heathens*, she'd say.

I googled *time travel*. It was what made the most sense, even if it didn't feel quite right, but nothing helpful came up. There was a lot that mentioned general relativity, quantum physics, and there were theories on what life would be like if we all had a time machine, but nothing compared to what I was experiencing now.

I flipped the coin again. *Memento mori.*

How could this be real? I swear, Bubba always had this on him, so how could I have it now? What was it doing on the ground in that place?

Eventually, I fell asleep. Grandmommy found me at some point, brought up a sandwich and smoothed my curls. I never touched the sandwich. It stayed on my bedside table, hardening. The better version of myself would be pissed I'd let food go to waste, but this version of myself felt like I was trapped in the jaws of the sea. Never moving forward.

My eyes snapped open every time Grandmommy checked on me. It was almost on the hour. She'd stand at the edge of my doorway, looking in with a stretched neck.

To both of our surprise, I was still here.

She decided I should stay home the next day, so I did, lying in bed still.

I googled the saying on the coin. It meant this: *Remember that you will die.*

EIGHT

Bubba was the worst at hide-and-seek, and when I turned eight, I wondered if he did it on purpose. He didn't hide in the den. Not in the basement, or in the closet behind the front door. Not in the small space behind the leather couch in the living room, or under his bed, or in the deepest darkest spot in the attic.

Instead, I'd find his colorful Huaraches peeking from beneath the long curtain in the living room, his body clearly bulging in the fabric, a laugh coming from him before I even approached.

He didn't try. He hid in plain sight, and it took away the fun of playing the game. My throat didn't squeeze with anxious breath. My fingertips weren't hot and tingling, awaiting the moment when I'd draw back a blanket to find that he wasn't there bundled in the pile of laundry on the floor in his bedroom.

My stomach didn't ripple like an angry wave being tossed by the tide as I crept around on the tips of my toes, careful not to cause a creak in the wood floors. All of it was mediocre, at best.

When I hid, I took the game seriously.

I could have been hidden for days, and no soul would find me. I found every corner, every crack, every hole in the house. If it was big enough for me to shimmy my way though, I'd get in there.

Eventually, though, I'd give up. Waiting would turn to minutes, and I'd find that Bubba was where he always was—either in the living room on his game, or in his room on his laptop.

He'd tell me he'd forgotten. *It was my bad, sissy,* he'd say, but I knew it was because he was bored of me. Mama tried to sit me down one day to explain that Bubba was fifteen now, becoming a man. Blah blah blah. She said he didn't want to play children's games anymore, but hiding wasn't *just* for kids. It was for everyone.

Today, Bubba was gone.

It had been two weeks since he went missing. We were at the house—Mama and Daddy packing a few personal items for all of us—and it was so cold I had to keep my coat on. The air felt odd and quiet. I didn't think it had ever really been this quiet. Daddy always had the TV on. Mama always had a client over, doing their hair in the kitchen while they cackled over something, and Bubba would yell. It was into his headset at his game, but he was distracted enough that I could sneak into his room and throw my stuffed animals at him.

Payback for ignoring me.

In this stillness, with sunlight peeking through the dusty windows, I wondered if Bubba was hiding.

I looked for him with a laugh in my heart, but there was an ominous and pulling feeling around every corner I turned. It was in the dimly lit hallway, between the kitchen and the living room, where I paused in my tracks.

Right at the tips of my toes and deep in the rug, there were thick burgundy dots splattered on the ground. A flash of a trigger being pulled. My bottom lip dropping as I stared at it for a long time. Then a slow *eeek* came, my bedroom door, farther down the hall, creaking until it came to a halt. A sliver of light poured in. A whisper of my name nearby.

I dashed to the door, my breath leaping. It could be Bubba.

My hand on the golden knob as I eased it open the rest of the way, looking, looking.

I spotted a shadow that zipped into the cracks of the room, dust filtering through the air as my chest rose, and my eyes searched and searched, but no one was in there. Not even another shadow.

Just my empty bedroom, exactly as I left it. A pillow on the floor. My bed almost made.

I huffed, leaving the room but still searching for him. I looked behind doors and couches, under beds and stairs. He wasn't behind the curtains giggling, waiting, and I refused to believe it.

Bubba couldn't be gone. Not really.

I still felt him in this place. Could sense the thumping of his heart, his warm breath, in these walls, behind the wallpaper. Somewhere close. He had to be hiding, waiting for me to find him.

And when I told my parents that very thing, Mama's eyes rounded, red breaking into the clear white, tears pooling in her rims.

"We just have to try," I pressed, my small voice rising.

We needed to open all the doors, turn on all the lights, look under everything. Would we forgive ourselves if we didn't? We'd spent so much time outside, knocking on doors, hanging up flyers, searching. Calling friends, tracking phones, driving around the block for hours. We didn't spend enough time *inside*. It was where we went when our legs were tired and our hearts were full and our brains were overworked. We laid our heads on pillows in this very place, so why wouldn't we look?

Daddy tugged on one of my braids. "Baby girl," he said, but it was all he could say. He scooped me in his arms, my chin on his shoulder as he carried me out of the house into the chilly

November air. The smell of frozen earth and smoke. Our little neighborhood seemed like a ghost town. Not even a stray cat running across the road.

I couldn't see Mama from here, but I could hear her struggling to breathe, could hear her chest breaking as she gasped for air, choking the tears out. And I closed my eyes, resting on Daddy, trying to pretend that none of this was happening.

NINE

PRESENT DAY: FEBRUARY

By Wednesday, I returned to school. In pottery class, Sarah sat beside me, hair pulled away from her face in a low ponytail. She teased as I tried to center my clay on the wheel.

"It's like a baby. You gotta coddle it better than that."

So I revved up the force—the clay suddenly forming at my will, until then it wasn't. It shifted past the center, away from me.

"I take it back. Less coddling. It's more like a boob."

I almost choked on my spit with a laugh, looking around to see if anyone else heard it. She looked with me, already knowing she was in the clear. I rolled my eyes and laughed again, stopping the wheel to pick up my clay and plop it back into the center.

With my foot on the pedal, the slow spin began again. The clay pushing into the center of my palm.

"Remember—*like a boob*," Sarah whispered.

"Will you stop with the boob analogy?"

She smirked.

"What do you mean, anyway?"

Her clay was already centered, and she was pulling it open with her fingers, forming a small bowl-like thing. "Haven't you been felt up? You want it to be rough, but not *too* rough. Gentle, but not *too* gentle."

I scrunched my nose and she elbowed me.

"It's been . . . a while." Half true. It *had* been a while, but the last time a dude tried to feel me up, it was one of my guy friends. It had been completely unwarranted, and I almost broke his fingers. Popped them at the knuckle.

I tried again with Sarah's advice. Balancing out the way my body was supposed to be. It was difficult—I wasn't used to working that muscle in my gut. After a few adjustments, the clay began to center. It was only slightly wobbly, and I cupped my palms around both sides of the clay mound, surprised that I'd done it.

"See, now you're an expert," she said, a dead-straight smile pinned on her face.

I rolled my eyes.

"Cool necklace." She nodded toward me as my necklace dangled over the pottery wheel. I'd forgotten it was there. Always on me, resting on my neck for the last two years. A gold best friend necklace. Half a crooked heart. Lucia had the other half. Made me miss Kansas City, and my old crew. And Lucia.

"Thanks," I said, and after class I checked my phone.

Still no response from Lucia. Her silence only confirmed my suspicion that something was up. Maybe she was afraid of me?

I hoped not. She was the only person I could talk to who would understand, and I wanted to tell her about this coin.

I texted her.

???

Girl!

Sorry. It's been hectic

See you Friday

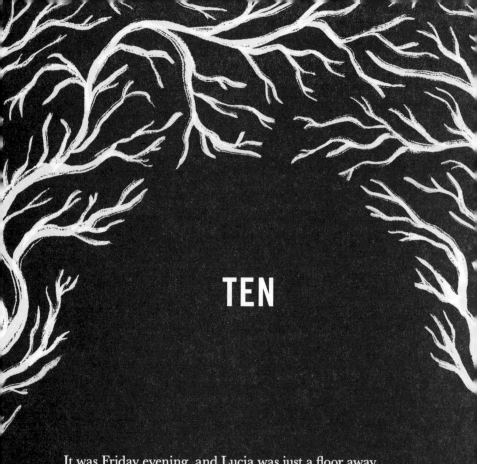

TEN

It was Friday evening, and Lucia was just a floor away.

Her mother's minivan had pulled into Grandmommy's driveway five minutes ago. Her mom was dropping her off so we could get ready together. Something we used to do before I moved to live with Grandmommy, and before she started going to parties without me. Before she thought my friends in my art classes were weird.

But Lucia had cousins who lived over here—probably the real reason she came—and her plan was to stay at their house so she could attend her baby cousin's dedication on Saturday.

Mrs. Rios had always been incredibly strict about Lucia staying anywhere, but if Lucia really wanted to stay the night at Grandmommy's, she would have found a way. She'd done it for her other friends.

I stretched my neck from the staircase to see Mrs. Rios at the door, talking to Grandmommy in a hushed voice, their whispers rising and stabbing at my ears.

Lucia was there, too, her head down, staring at her phone with her pink duffel bag draped across her shoulders. She was waiting to be released. It was Mrs. Rios's thing. She had to wait. She had to listen. Then, when it was time, they'd say good-bye.

The stairs moaned as I stretched farther, and everyone looked up at me—brown eyes glowing in yellow light and fading sun.

"Mi amor, come down here and give me a hug," Mrs. Rios said.

I released a deep sigh as I trudged down the last few steps because *shit*. She knew. I knew she knew by the wavering in her voice. It was like Mama's. It was like Daddy's. And she'd probably been talking to Grandmommy about it, probably asking if I was "okay."

That was what people wanted to know when something strange happened to you. They wanted to know if you were okay. But even if you weren't okay, even if you had blood seeping from your nostrils, even if you were afraid and confused, they didn't know how to help.

This was what I was learning. The world was only artificially safe.

Mrs. Rios's arms were stretched out, and Grandmommy moved out of the way to let me through. I pressed myself into her, staring at Lucia's crooked smile all the while, trying to wordlessly communicate: *What the hell did you say to your mom????*

Lucia raised her shoulders slightly, the big bun on the top of her head wobbling. Her mom squeezed me tight, patting my head. She smelled of roses with sharp thorns.

"Hylee, don't be a stranger," Mrs. Rios said. It sounded more like a warning, and I wanted to roll my eyes, but that would have been rude. Then she released me. "Abuelita has been asking about you."

I hid my gaze. "I'll have to visit soon." I winced as I said it. It wasn't that I was on lockdown—it was more or less that Grandmommy had been watching me like a hawk since Monday, requesting I text her on my way to and from school. It was a surprise she'd let me go to this party tonight. Probably because Lucia would be there, and also probably because I hadn't disappeared in four days.

I stood next to Grandmommy with a forced smile on my face. No one said anything for a few moments, and it made the air thick. Guessed they didn't want to talk about me now that I was here.

Mrs. Rios turned to Lucia with a breath. "Pues, I'll text you later, Luciana. You better text me back," she said, giving her a smothering hug and a kiss. Something Mama used to do to me. Especially right after Bubba went missing. She was shaking when she hugged me last week, bags beneath her eyes.

"*Mommy*, okay, okay. I will." Lucia broke away from her mother, crossing the threshold.

I followed, passing her and heading up the stairs. When we got to my room, she rushed to the window, dropping her bag on the bed.

She turned, and I noticed the obvious. She wasn't wearing her best friend necklace I'd gotten her for her quince. My neck and chest burned from where mine resided. I'd saved up so much babysitting money from the summer before. And still. *Still*...

I didn't know why it was bothering me now. Maybe because everything was fucking bothering me. But she never wore the stupid thing anyway, and my fingers tingled.

I was so tempted to rip mine away from my neck. And I couldn't ask her why she didn't wear it. I couldn't. She'd think I was obsessed or some shit, and I *wasn't* obsessed. I just didn't know why she didn't care.

"Loving this view." Her voice broke through, my vision refocusing as she pressed her fingers to the window, pointing to something.

Twisted my lips, the bottom one peeling, and that bothered me, but it was my silence that made her turn. Her shoulders dropped. *"What?"*

"Nothing."

She leaned her head to the side. Maybe a little confused at first, and then it clicked. "Okay. Here we go lying."

"Well, obviously it's not nothing. I feel like you've been MIA since I disappeared."

Her mouth popped open like one of those baby dolls with a hole carved out for a bottle, and it looked like she wanted to say something, but she didn't. She just stood there.

"And did you tell your mom?!"

Lucia rolled her eyes. "Girl, calm down."

I leaned forward. "Calm down???" My chest rose in quick beats, my ears warm. "Did you tell anyone else?"

"No." She looked at me. "And why can't I tell my mom? You know I tell her everything." Translation: *Just because you're not as close to your mom doesn't mean it's weird for me to be close to my mom.*

It wasn't weird, but it *was* a jab.

I wanted to take her bag and throw it out the window. I was close enough, my toe pressing into the side of the fabric. But I felt lightheaded. I unballed my fists. "It's not that I don't want you to tell your mom—I don't want you to tell *anyone*. I don't even know what's happening to me, and I don't need everyone's eyes on me.

And I needed you. This whole time you've been ignoring me, I needed you. You're my best friend, and you were there that night, and my family can't even look at me."

Lucia plopped on the bed with a deep sigh, her bun bouncing, her eyes wandering to the window. "Girl...I'm sorry," she said, but neither of us moved. Wished I could break the window. She wasn't sorry. She just didn't want to talk about it.

I groaned. I didn't want to talk about it anymore, either. It wasn't worth it.

Lucia turned to stare at me, eyes round. She knew the fight was over because she wanted it to be. Then she smiled a little, opening her arms for a hug.

I was hesitant, but I joined her anyway. We hugged for a few seconds, and then she said: "I—I needed to process what happened. I mean, I don't even know what happened. It all kind of feels like a blur. Plus, you know how it is. I've been...busy. I have to keep my grades up for the KC Scholars program. I need that money for college."

I didn't say anything, and Lucia sighed. "Can I be honest? I'm not sure I even know what happened that night. Truth. It was already a long-ass day for me, and you know Abuelita hasn't been feeling well, and really, I was running on, like, three hours of sleep that day. I'm just...I'm not sure what I saw. I remembered you weren't there, and then, all of a sudden, you were. In my head, I pieced together that you weren't feeling well. You said it earlier that day yourself—didn't you have a migraine? So maybe you left the living room and you blacked out. And maybe I just didn't see you get up to leave."

Even if that were all-the-way true, it didn't explain the coin. It didn't explain how I disappeared and returned. It didn't explain the barely tolerable gnawing in the back of my throat—my desire to yell and be heard. It didn't explain my own name on repeat inside me. How could I brush any of those things off and narrow it down to a migraine?

It had happened, and I knew I was right. I knew I was.

But the more I let it sit with me, the more I didn't know anymore.

Maybe it *was* all in my head. Maybe it had never happened.

And if it had happened, maybe it was something I couldn't share with Lucia anymore.

ELEVEN

When the sun dipped down past the hills, Lucia got a text saying that her cousins—Carmen, Rae, and Jess (Carmen's on-again/off-again girlfriend)—were here.

I was crammed in the backseat of a Ford Taurus, gripping the chicken handle as we flew around each corner, the force of it smashing me into the door each time. Swear, I didn't know if her brakes were bad or if she just didn't use them, but by some miracle we made it.

Apparently, there was a girl named Kesha who went to my

school. This was her house party, and her parents lived in one of the newer homes in this neighborhood behind Brindleton Bay.

Also apparently, her parents owned five restaurants in the area, and her dad was a partner at a personal injury firm in downtown KC.

"They have money," Lucia had said once we all climbed out of the car. We had to park farther away because her driveway already had cars lined up bumper to bumper.

The front door was unlocked when we got to it, and taped below the peephole was a sign that read PARTY IN BASEMENT.

Did people really leave their doors unlocked here? Maybe they just weren't as paranoid as my family was. Daddy made sure we had three locks on the door wherever we moved to. But the thing about locks was that they had the potential to keep you in just as much as they could keep you out.

I followed the group of giggling girls through another door and then down a set of steps.

A mix of food and sweet tobacco rose to meet me as I descended the staircase.

When I got to the last step, I could see the light blue paint on the walls and the tiny, twinkling lights that dangled from corner to corner. Some boys on the couch beside the stairs bounced up and down on the cushions, roaring out lyrics to the song that played.

Past the group of boys, I followed Lucia and her cousins over to a table in the far corner. There were food and drinks, and it was something to be doing instead of standing here looking dumb as hell.

A lot of these kids went to my school. I could see that now. And I'd wondered where the Brown and Black kids hung out—it was something about those hallways that drowned us out and made us feel like colored specks in a cup of milk.

"Will you please check my tooth?" Lucia pulled me to the side while her cousins grabbed drinks. "I swear something is in there. I can feel it right here." She pointed to one of her front teeth, but nothing was there.

"I don't see anything, Lucia."

Her lips folded into a pout, and I focused my attention on the growing crowd.

"Are you still mad at me?" she whispered, but it wasn't really a whisper, not with this loud music.

I could've said yes, and normally I would have, but it wouldn't have changed anything. Not anymore. So I said, "No," because that was easier. In the same way that ignoring that I'd suddenly vanished in thin air was easier for her. I know, I know. It was petty. But that was how you won at being a liar—you had to be petty.

Lucia sighed. "Okay."

People spilled from the stairway, huddling in groups around the room. A few kids over by the back door gathered around a hookah thing. Dudes in groups of four and five held up the back wall like it would absolutely fall without them. Lots of hand rubbing, lip licking. Waiting.

Coming toward me, a Black girl with a bright smile, fresh Marley twists, and a strapless red dress. I squinted, realizing who it was, and then smiled. It was my cousin Asia.

"Cousin, what are you doing here?" We hugged, and she smelled like what I imagined Rihanna smelled like.

Asia wiggled her shoulders, her dark brown skin shimmering from the body glitter. "I know people," she said, and honestly, she really did. Asia had a big social media following, and people were always inviting her to parties.

"Did you come by yourself?"

Her glossed pout and lip liner thinned into a smirk. "Girl, naw! You know my mama would be mad if I came all the way out here by myself. I came with Imani. She's over there talking to some guy she knows." Asia pointed to the crowd that was growing by the steps, and I could sort of see Imani whispering into someone's ear over the music. Imani and Asia had been inseparable since they'd joined the drill team together.

"I'm surprised to see you here. Sis, you never go to parties."

I forced a smile, and at the same time, Lucia brought me a red plastic cup. "Drink up, buttercup."

I sniffed it. "What's in it?"

"Jungle juice, I think. Oh, hey, Asia! It's great seeing you," Lucia said, giving Asia a hug. They talked, and I took one sip. Then two. Three sips, then four. It tasted like fruit punch, but with tangerine and something I couldn't name.

Lucia's cousins crowded around us. Then Imani came over. One of the Black girls in my grade came over, too. We talked for a while about school. How she grew up around here. How she was planning on going to UMKC.

Seconds turned into minutes and the girls were laughing around me, and I laughed, too. Not because I was listening, but just so that I could feel like I was part of the conversation.

The problem was, I felt a haze filtering over my eyes, like I was dreaming, breathing deep and even. In my mind, all I could see was that little girl's face again. I saw the way her vined lips kept twisting, like, even if she wanted to speak, she couldn't. It was as if she were here, in this room, joining the chorus of my name on repeat in my mind and the hands . . . the hands that were coming for me but never close enough to grab me.

Another sip. Another sip.

"Hylee?"

I jerked, my knees buckling a little.

Asia was really close to me. "Hey, did you hear me? Will you snap this photo of me and Imani real quick?"

My eyelids fluttered, and I focused my gaze. The girl wasn't here. The hands weren't after me. The voice in my head didn't exist. "Yeah, of course." She handed me her phone, and I set my drink down, following them to a wall of lights. A few cute poses later, and they were all done. Handed the phone back and stayed behind, under the twinkling lights, listening to the music.

And then, like the pivotal point in a story, it happened: Some boy was staring at me. Not the creepy kind of stare, but one where his brown eyes pooled like honey in this dim light. Where his mouth was draped with a slanted smile like we'd just shared an inside joke. His nose ring caught the light as he moved, and he was looking at me.

A look I felt I knew.

He was in the center of the crowd, speaking to someone now, and even when Lucia and her girls came over to laugh about something that happened, he still stuck out like a sore thumb. Tall. Curly hair. Full lips.

He greeted someone else. They dapped, they shared quick conversation, but he held my stare. Even from all the way over there, he was fixated on me, and I had to look over my shoulder solely to make sure it wasn't my cousin, my friend, or anyone else, but it wasn't. Only me.

Time slowed as he pivoted in the crowd, narrowing himself to get past people, and it felt like I'd known him somehow, like I could see every memory of us. A blurry, sped-up version of him holding my hand. Of me, touching his brown face. Of us, smashing our lips into each other, our noses only a hair away from rubbing. It was like I could *smell* him—sweet sandalwood and spice.

Journeys end in lovers meeting.

But I didn't know him. I didn't.

I looked away from him, ignoring the shifting behind my eyes. The jungle juice was setting in quicker than I thought it would.

I pressed my arms against my center, and I listened to Lucia tell a story. One I'd heard before. One I'd heard a lot, actually. It was Lucia's thing. She liked to retell stories. Sometimes because she'd forget, or sometimes she'd do it because she liked talking about it so much. I didn't mind, though. Stories were what kept us alive.

But my thoughts wondered about the boy again, and I glanced into the crowd, just for a moment, just to see if he was still there.

He was, and he was coming toward me, gliding past the people like they were frozen around him. And I felt like I couldn't breathe because what the hell would I say when he made it over here? *HI?*

My freaking out didn't stop him, though. After only a few seconds, he was a foot away from me, taller than me, wearing that smile and making me wish I could splinter into the wood of this floor.

"Hey," he said, his voice soft, a little raspy.

My throat suddenly felt dry, my heart squeezing.

I wondered what I looked like to him. Brown-skinned. Big hair.

Barely breathing correctly in this black dress that belonged to Lucia and fit her frame much better than it would ever fit mine. It was because of my boobs. They were just too big for this thing. I'd tried squishing them down, so they would fit, but these spaghetti straps were doing overtime. Lucia told me I looked great, but I didn't know what to believe from her.

"Hey," I said, and the girls stopped talking and giggling to see what was happening. He noticed, looking at them and holding up a hand to say hi.

"Heeey," they said in unison, stretching the word into two syllables instead of one. We all stared at him. Some of us with smiles. And then. That raspy voice again, cracking through the music and words. A whiff of coffee coming with it. "If it's cool with you all, may I talk with . . . ? He paused to look at me.

"May I?" Asia cut in. "Boy, you talk like you're from the eighteenth century."

He slowly looked at me. Then his eyes lowered.

"Anyway, her name's Hylee, Mr. May I," Asia continued.

"Thanks, Asia, but I can speak for myself," I said between my teeth. Lucia shoved me in the shoulder, and then I looked at him, my vision a little hazy, my stomach tight. "Are you sure it's me you want to talk to?" I asked, and it wasn't a bad question. I looked good, but I couldn't remember the last time some dude approached me at a party. But also, for that to happen I guessed I'd have to actually *go* to parties.

A smile appeared. "Yeah, I mean. If that's cool?"

"Yeah, it's cool," Asia answered. Asia was born impatient, so she shoved her way over to us, wrapping her arm around my shoulder and his shoulder and pushing us away from the group of girls. Then she waved like a princess and flipped her Marley twists away from her shoulder, like she was one of those white kids visiting the city and leaving after a few hours of volunteer work. Bet her heart was all warm inside.

"Have fun!" It was the last thing she said before she walked away.

The room swallowed us in its loudness, and I smiled with dead eyes, still unsure of how I came to be standing, alone, with this boy.

As interesting as it was that he wanted to talk to me, he didn't say anything. At least, not at first. He acted just as awkward as I felt, letting that silence sink into our veins, and trying not to stare at me, though it was obvious he couldn't stop.

"Did you know E.E. Cummings was the first person to use the term *party* as a verb? It was in some letter he wrote about how he *partied* in Paris in 1920."

I squinted. "So that's your opening line?"

He stared at me, a smile spreading.

"How do you even know that?" I asked.

He shrugged. "I googled it."

"*Why?*"

"Why not?"

"Do we know each other?" I blurted out, because the question needed to be asked. We were standing here, face-to-face, like we knew each other, and I didn't think we did.

It seemed like he wanted to shake his head, but then he raised a finger, a smile in the corner of his lips. "See, I wanted to ask you that. You seem so familiar, but when I approached you, I realized I didn't know your name. My bad if I made you feel uncomfortable. I just swore I knew you from somewhere."

"Oh."

"Yeah."

Silence between us again, and the glowing lights blurred behind him like a camera lens opening too slow. I imagined this moment was what the beginning and ending of an indie film looked like— all sentimental with some folky song unfolding into existence. Something my art friends back home would gawk over with drool sliding down the corners of their lips, while I'd probably roll my eyes. Not because it wasn't cool, but because it was overrated. I hated that I was like that sometimes.

Fine. I hated that I was like that *most* times.

My weight shifted from one side of my body to the other, and I felt wobbly. How much jungle juice did I have?

"Do you like to dance?"

"Why? Do you have a fun fact about that, too?"

I stared at his dark pink lips while he spoke, another smile sneaking into the corners, like he was holding something back. But I wanted in on whatever the secret was. "Actually," he started, and I wanted to nudge him in the shoulder. I didn't. It would be weird; we didn't know each other. "Did you know dance has been around since before written language? Some say celebratory dancing was essential to the development of early human civilization."

"How do you know this?"

He shrugged again. "We have access to everything we want to know at our fingertips."

My focus was on his neck now, the way he swallowed. Afraid of me almost. It made me smile, and I looked away from him, my chest warm. "I don't like dancing in public. I don't want people assuming I can dance just because I'm Black."

He chuckled. "Yeah, me either."

"So wait, what was your name? I never got it."

"I'm Eilam."

I leaned against what I thought was a wall but turned out to be an end table. I wobbled and then fell right on top of it, hearing the sound of thread ripping a little under my armpit. Shit. I hoped I didn't ruin Lucia's dress.

"Woah, you good?" he asked, his hand cool against my forearm, helping me up. My body felt like it was on fire. He made sure I was firmly planted before he completely let go.

"Yeah, I'm fine. I just thought the wall was there—"

"No, sorry. I was talking to the table." He moved past me to pat the top of the wooden surface that had survived the destruction. "Are *you* okay?" he asked, bending his knees to get closer to the table. He looked at me. "Uh, I think he's broken. Can't seem to respond to my question."

I laughed, my eyes squinting a little. "Nice joke."

"I like your laugh," he said.

I pressed my lips together, the gloss sticking. The last time I was in a relationship with someone was a year ago. It was a long-distance relationship with one of Lucia's cousins. I'd met him at this family kick-back. That lasted for a month, but besides the thrill of texts, and one odd, and very vivid, inappropriate pic, there wasn't much else there.

"Do you need some water?"

"I should probably drink some," I admitted, still feeling my center shifting back and forth.

Eilam looked behind me, and by the way his nose scrunched,

I could tell he was thinking of something. "Okay, you stay right here. I'm going to go get you some—"

"Actually." I touched his shoulder, and my thighs tingled. It stopped him, and we stared at each other, swallowing at the same time before I remembered what I was going to say. "Can I go with? I need some air."

"Yeah—yeah. Of course." He extended a hand, and I took it, his fingers cupping mine, molding perfectly. "Follow me," he said.

I didn't know if it was the alcohol, or the lights in the background, but in those few seconds, I was reminded of the last clip in *Titanic*. The one where Jack Dawson stands at the top of the staircase, with the grand clock in the background, and holds his hand out, waiting for Rose. He had been waiting all that time for her, and they were finally together again, for the first time, in an alternate universe.

It was definitely the alcohol.

Definitely.

But that was what this felt like.

TWELVE

Eilam watched me down two straight bottles of water outside of Kesha's house.

"Save some for the fish," he mumbled as I guzzled down the rest of the last one. He stared at me like I was a balancing act in the circus, standing a bit too close, as if to catch me if I lost my balance.

I took one wobbly step back, trying to prove a point.

When I finished, I shoved both empty bottles into his chest. "Please find a place to recycle these. The world is already a mess as it is."

"Fact. Humans are an ecological catastrophe," he said, cupping the bottles in both arms like he was holding a baby.

Around me, this little neighborhood blended into the night, and I still couldn't wrap my head around the fact that I was out here, living in a neighborhood like *this*. The earth smelled like wet wood. The air pressed against my skin like small pins, pricking at the surface.

Out here, they were in the process of building homes. Homes that families would soon live in. Families like mine used to look like, and I wondered if the families that lived here were ever ripped apart. Certainly. Not even the rich could afford a painless life. But at least they could cover it up with dollar bills and health insurance. Could you imagine what my life would be like if I were in therapy? No? Well, me either.

Farther out, in the shadows behind the streetlights, I could see something darker than the night moving like long tentacles against the ground.

It made a thick lump form in the back of my throat as I remembered the dark place, its strangeness, and the little girl with skin so thin her eyes were skeletal and deep and dark.

Each time I tried to swallow, I felt myself losing air.

Swallow. Swallow. Swallow. Don't think.

But as the world became hazier, all I could *do* was think. Flashes of the dark place. A scream piercing my chest. The sound of something thick slithering on the floor. A trigger, and metal releasing a bang.

I finally swallowed. A gasp almost. Eilam looked at me with his brow furrowed as I said, "I should probably sit," holding my arms and feeling a partition forming within me—almost like someone cracking an egg slowly, waiting for the yolk to spill out.

A mess. I was a mess.

He spoke a little too slow for my liking, like he was afraid I was fragile. "We can sit in my car if you want."

"No offense, but you're a stranger, and I don't exactly trust you enough to get in your car."

Eilam nodded, naked branches rustling against the sky above him. "Fair point. Um, okay, compromise. We can sit *on* my car."

I agreed, following him to a white Pontiac Sunfire with a dent in the fender. He patted the hood as a greeting, and then he sat. I copied, leaving space between us and staring up at the black sky, the Big Dipper scooping away at the universe. Could it scoop away at me, too?

"Have you always lived in Lee's Summit?"

My head spun as I tried to focus on him. He rippled in and out like sound waves, and the movement made my head feel like it was ticking. "Nope. Just moved here. I'm from Kansas City, Kansas."

The words came out, but it felt like there was air trapped in the back of my throat, like if I gasped right now, I wouldn't stop.

A grin. "Oh, so you're from *Kansas*."

"Don't be like that. There is nothing wrong with Kansas."

"Y'all got tumbleweed in Kansas."

I almost laughed, remembering the literal cows in front of my school. "You've clearly never been to Wyandotte County. It's more like tumble*weave*."

Eilam laughed, and I felt my stomach twist into the tightest knot. "That was good. You're funny. But I've been down there. I have an auntie who lives out by the Legends."

I cleared my throat. "What about you? Have you always lived here in Lee's Summit?" I asked.

"I live in Grandview. Not too far from here, but yeah. I grew up there."

Grandview...I didn't recognize the name, but maybe it was a neighborhood around here.

"What high school do you go to?" I hadn't seen him around my school, but there were so many people at my new school, I wouldn't be surprised if I'd missed him.

"I go to Grandview High School."

I nodded in response and recrossed my arms, feeling a numbing sensation beneath my nail beds. "What's that like?"

"Uh." A chuckle. "I mean I'm not quite sure what to compare it to, but it's different than Lee's Summit West, I can tell you that."

Was that a hint of animosity, or was I making that up? I was probably making it up, but... "In what way?"

His eyes glimmered. Were my words slurred? With my world spinning, I couldn't read him. "I like my school. And my neighborhood." He looked around. "I'm just saying it's different than this. Out here. I feel less displaced...."

Nodded. Straight smile. Okay. I saw what he was getting at. He didn't have to be so indirect about it. It wasn't like I couldn't relate, but he didn't know that. "So there are more Black kids at your school?"

"Bingo."

I laughed, but then I stopped myself because suddenly it felt like I was underwater.

Pressure coming in at me on all sides. My ears popping, and I felt so alone.

Alone, drowning. In my body, drowning.

Eilam said something, but it was hard to make out what it was because of the growing tingling that shot up my legs, turning me inside out.

He spoke again, and I caught broken fragments of it this time. "...can I...number? Hylee...all right?...safe...okay?" His eyes were all I could focus on. These big, brown things rounding and rounding. Like he was seconds away from shouting for help. And he was afraid. So was I.

Reached my hand toward him, warmth inches away from my fingertips. Thought I was grabbing at nothing at first, and then he handed me his phone.

My jaw numbing, but the weight of the device woke me a little. Called myself, feeling like I was about to tip over, thud against the roof of this car, and that was when I realized it wasn't the alcohol. It was me, my body about to vanish.

I shuddered with fear of what would come next.

Almost gone, I grabbed the wrist of his bomber, hoping it would ground me here, that I wouldn't go. And his mouth gaped, trying to—I think—keep me from falling.

But I couldn't make it stop. And he couldn't make it stop. This was bigger than us.

My grasp loosened, and I heard a flickering. The sound reminded me of a bug running into a porch light over and over again. Inevitable death.

A spark inside me, nausea rushing in.

And with an inhale, I thought I'd fallen against the car.

But when I reopened my eyes, I was back.

Back at my childhood home.

Back in the dark.

THIRTEEN

The darkness wrapped itself around me like a tourniquet, pressing into me until I felt my heartbeat throbbing against my neck.

The emerald streetlight brightened the dark path before me, and I followed the trail of light with my eyes, recognizing where I was.

Home again, at the end of the corroding driveway, back in Kansas City.

The thing about this driveway was that there was no definite beginning and ending. You pulled in at the front of the house, but if you continued, you'd follow the driveway down a slight hill, past the back porch, that flickering light, the gazebo, that tree, the backyard, and to the iron gate with the spikes that was stuck open at all times.

My childhood home was on a corner lot, so once you'd reached the end of the driveway, it would just take you back on the street again. You could keep coming and going, and going, and going if you wanted to. Infinite loops round and round.

Ahead, the darkness was thick. A movement, a shadow maybe. And if this was the same as last time, that terrifying girl would be coming again, and no way was I about to stay here and wait for that shit. *Nope.* No.

I started up the hill, toward the brown house with the white-painted windows that looked like eyes, watching my every movement. Mama and Daddy used to say that this was their forever home. It was hard to imagine that now. Home felt like an illusion here on Earth. So did "forever."

The back porch only had two steps up it, and beside the porch light there was a back door. I tried it, twisting the knob and pulling, but it was locked.

There were two windows that overlooked the back porch. One was connected to my old bedroom; I could climb in. It was something I'd done before. Whenever Bubba and I would play flashlight tag with our friends, and I'd get tired, I'd sneak back inside, calling it a night.

Pressed my fingers against the cool glass, my eyes closed tight as I pushed upward, hoping. It was stiff at first, but eventually the window glided up the track, the warmer inside air blowing against my chest. The smell of something I knew, sweet and warm, and the smell of something else, rusting metal and damp carpet.

My heart screamed at me to run, to turn around. But where would I go? And what if there was something here that I needed to find, like the coin? What if there was something else that could bring me to Bubba, help me figure out where he went?

From here, the blinds swaying in front of me, I could see that it was dark, but what exactly would be inside once I climbed in? Would that girl be there? Or something else—something *worse*?

Behind me, the night was still empty, quiet. Too quiet. The tree near the corner of the gazebo still stretched its limbs further than it should have. And if I waited . . .

But I didn't want to wait.

I hoisted myself up, pressing my shoes against the house paneling. A tear, and it made my heart skip a beat, but it was only the side of this black dress. Shit, I hoped Lucia would forgive me, because this thing would be trash after this.

Pushed past the blinds, and I slid to the carpeted floor as quietly as I could, surrounded by more darkness. Tried not to breathe too hard as my eyes adjusted.

A little away from me, to the right and on a nightstand, was an alarm clock I recognized. I perked up. There *was* more here. That alarm clock had been mine—it was a Disney-themed one that Daddy had gotten for my birthday one year, and in the brightest red, it displayed the date and the time.

Oh my God. Oh my God.

The alarm clock, the coin.

It still didn't make sense, though. When we left this house after the incident nine years ago, Mama said the bank foreclosed on us, and they had a big dump truck throw out everything we left behind—our pictures, our beds, our clothes. Some things I wished I still had.

But if my old alarm clock was here, then this place I was in, whatever it was, it couldn't be the present day. I wasn't just thrown back to Kansas City; I was thrown back to the past.

I closed my eyes, the bright red from the clock disappearing. I tried to pretend that Mama and Daddy were here sleeping and that Bubba was in his room playing his Xbox and that my world was okay.

But something told me I should keep my eyes open. I looked at the clock once more. The date and time: November 9.

The date was familiar, but I couldn't remember why.

November 9, November 9, November 9.

And in the quickest of beats, I heard a swift inhale and exhale.

Sweet and sour. The breath was shaky, uneven, like someone was huffing and scared. Someone breathing in and out through their nose. Someone panicking.

To my left.

Something to my left.

When I looked, she was there.

The light from the porch seeped through the blinds to reveal the little girl with no eyes. She was hunched in a squatting position beside me, breathing deeply, her nostrils flaring as her chest rattled.

Before I caught my breath to scream, her little hand covered my mouth, scaring me out of existence. And I remembered what happened on November 9. It was the day Bubba disappeared.

FOURTEEN

PRESENT DAY: FEBRUARY

Back.

I was back in Lee's Summit, my chest rising and falling in quick beats as the cool air rushed against my cheeks.

I knew it was the present because of where I lay on the ground. The trees looked familiar. The thinned branches poked into the night. The same streetlights. I could even hear the bass from the music echoing against the empty evening, absorbing into the earth.

My body was wet and sticky from the damp, cold ground, and when I sat up, I threw up immediately. It was a sign. I swore I'd never drink alcohol again. But that was probably another lie.

I got to my feet and wiped my mouth, pissed and disgusted with myself. Because why, *why* was this happening to me? Why did I keep disappearing? Why did I keep getting taken away from the moment I was in?

And more. What was up with that house—all of our things there—and that girl?

I wanted to be anchored here, in the present...but also, I wanted to know why this was happening to me.

I was at the corner of Kesha's yard, by her curved driveway, and no one else was around. Many of the cars that were here earlier were gone, including Eilam's white Pontiac.

How much time had passed, and what would he think of me? There was no way I could explain myself, and even if I did, he'd probably be too terrified to listen, too terrified to look in my brown eyes and *see* me. It would be a repeat of the Lucia situation all over again. And I'd have to lie to him, somehow make him think that none of this happened.

Lucia. Was she still here? Was she looking for me?

Rushed into the house, my right leg limping as the tingling worked its way down my thigh, slowly going away.

In the basement, the crowd was much smaller than before, the music more relaxed. A group of kids chilled on the couch by the stairs, and a couple slow danced in the center of the room. No one turned their heads or looked my way as I passed them.

In the back corner, resting on the edge of the food table that looked completely run over, was my bag. Someone must have picked it up and left it there.

Scrambled for my phone as my eyes blurred.

I had a few missed calls from a number I didn't recognize. A text from Grandmommy asking when I'd be home, and eight missed texts from Lucia.

Each text worsened as they progressed.

At first it was concern, and then there was the assumption that I'd run away with Eilam.

She said she'd left. That my cousin left. They all left, and no one waited around for me.

No one waited. Didn't they care?

I took off after that, leaving Kesha's house and entering the dark, my phone to my ear. Lucia's line rang and rang, but she didn't answer. I tried to blink away the tears, but I knew. In my heart, I knew this was probably the last straw for her.

She wouldn't believe me if I told her I'd disappeared again. Not only because she couldn't handle the disappearing—but because who would believe a liar? And in the back of my throat, I knew it wasn't just that. It was everything.

I could tell myself that all my lies catered to her need—no, her intense craving—for normalcy, but was that even true? Didn't I also lie to protect myself, to keep her by my side? Eventually, I knew, there would come a time when lies weren't enough, but I hadn't thought that would be today.

And the realization that she was probably done with me forever made me choke.

I gasped for air as I walked, wiping away my tears and almost falling to my knees. I had let down my best friend, and she'd never want anything to do with me ever again.

My sobs were so loud in this darkness. The dead neighborhood, sitting in mocking silence. A vision of that girl in the back of my head. My world in disarray. No one to acknowledge it but me.

A few twisted shadows nearby, lingering by the construction. It was three in the morning, and Grandmommy's house was only a mile away, in the neighborhood behind here, and after I undid my strappy sandals, I started moving, afraid that if I stood still for too long, I'd see those shadows move, and I'd hear breathing close to my neck.

Tied my curls into a bun, my bangs frizzy and floppy against my forehead. Jogged the entirety, my borrowed dress still splitting in the spots it had earlier, and adrenaline pushing me through as my toes scraped the concrete. The angry morning tickled the back of my calves, kissed my tears.

As I ran, I kept thinking about Lucia and Eilam and that house. The girl. The past. Why I was there.

November 9 was the day Bubba disappeared, but my memory of what happened was broken. Why was the past forcing me to return to such a horrid day?

But it wasn't just the past. It was more than that. The past didn't have monsters.

The door creaked when I entered the house. Grandmommy was as much a heavy sleeper as Daddy was. They could sleep through literal fire alarms, which was dangerous and just ridiculous. Today, I guessed, it was a good thing. I didn't want to be grounded for being out so late.

I spent longer than usual in the shower. Crying and deep conditioning my hair. I should have detangled it, but I barely had the energy to do anything more than simply be here. Something I'd surely regret tomorrow, but it was all I had in me at the moment.

After my shower, I twisted my wet curls into an old T-shirt to dry and got in my pj's. Then I texted Lucia.

Lucia, I'm so sorry

It was all I could say. Even if we were done, she had to know. Maybe she'd respond, but the chances were slim.

Lucia held grudges better than anyone I knew. A couple

summers ago, we had a crush on the same guy. When he asked me on a date, she didn't talk to me for the rest of the summer.

Not that I was sinless. I accepted the date. I kissed the boy. I lied until I was caught. And I did it because it was the first thing I had outside Lucia. Someone who gave me attention, even if it was for all the wrong reasons.

I was selfish, and I wanted him. And he wanted me, and I needed that.

So it was my fault. I begged and begged for forgiveness. Sent text after text, and she probably laughed. Showed her other friends how pathetic I was (side note: I was). Not to wallow in self-pity, but I had been a shitty friend.

And today, again, it was my fault. Partly.

I couldn't control what was happening to me, but I was already at the point of no return before that, and thinking about what I'd already done to Lucia, could I blame her for not wanting to be my friend? It'd be so easy to lie and say *of course*. But *I* wouldn't even want to be my friend, even if I felt bad for me, and knowing that . . . it hurt like hell.

The unknown number that had texted and called earlier was Eilam. I'd given him my phone number right before I disappeared.

> Hey this is Eilam

> It feels kind of ridiculous for me to ask if you're okay

But are you okay?

This sounds even worse

but I hope you aren't dead

I'm alive

Sorry if I scared you

FIFTEEN

My guilt and fear kept me awake.

Red-stained eyes and a wet pillowcase. I tossed and turned, restless. I kept waking up, trying to erase the vision of monsters in my head. I turned on the lamp to push away the darkness, and I grabbed for my phone.

I went to Google for answers. I wanted to know more. I searched my old address, and Google Maps showed me an image of it.

There it was, standing somberly on the street corner. Abandoned and alone, in clear disrepair. Looking at it made me feel sick. After a while, I tried to look up information about what happened in Kansas City, Kansas, on November 9.

At first, I couldn't find anything—which, nothing to be surprised about—but then I stumbled across an article:

KANSAS CITY, Kan.—Kansas City Police are investigating a break-in and deadly shooting Sunday night.

Neighbors say they heard gunshots at around 10:15 p.m.

Upon arrival, officers located an unresponsive man suffering from gunshot wounds.

EMS responded and declared the victim deceased at the scene.

Police reported several occupants of the home fled the scene, but a minor was discovered hiding in the bathroom. The minor was uninjured.

The family says they are still missing their son, Eugene Williams Jr., who is believed to have fled the scene as well. The boy is 15 years of age and is described as Black with brown skin. He was last seen wearing dark jeans and a graphic T-shirt.

Detectives and crime scene personnel are processing

the scene to get more information about what led to the shooting and break-in.

Anyone with information is asked to call the Kansas City Police Department or the anonymous TIPS Hotline.

My eyes skipped over words while I read. My throat closed in on itself. And then I read it again and again until the words made sentences, and I could understand the paragraphs.

Reading the article almost made me numb. I saved it, shocked that someone could document a tragic event of my life in less than a page.

I opened a new tab and searched *alternate universes*. The first search result led to a Reddit link, and it seemed promising because this guy went into great detail about how he'd accidentally slipped into an alternate universe, but I got to the end and discovered he'd made the entire thing up. What a waste of time.

I thumbed my way down to the next post, and each story got darker and darker. Stories that felt like they were diary entries with twists that ended up like *Law and Order: SVU*. Stuff that shouldn't be on the internet at all, and the comments were just plain awful. Some of the worst advice I'd seen in my life.

When I plugged my phone back into the charger, I turned off the light and lay on my back, eyes to the white ceiling, wondering about my family and our seemingly terrible line of history. Something I kept pushing to the back of my mind.

It felt like the universe had always been against us, and I couldn't help but wonder if it had any connection to why I was being jerked through time and space.

Grandmommy only had one kid. She'd said the doctors told her it was because of the way her uterus was shaped, which meant she couldn't hold a baby to term. Said she was on bed rest with my daddy for three months before she delivered him early. Even after he was born, she'd told me she couldn't sleep at night; she was so worried, she'd wake up every hour just to make sure he was still breathing, just to make sure he was still there.

And I didn't know much about my great-grandparents or their parents.

Grandmommy wouldn't talk about her parents because they'd been estranged from her before they passed away, but despite that, I knew her mother had been adopted from a family we knew nothing about.

Mama had a similar issue. Not that she'd kept her side a secret, but that, along the way, she'd somehow forgotten the stories that were told, the ones that helped tell us who we were. My family's lineage could be summed up as dust in the wind, and it hurt not being able to have a heritage to brag about, a legacy to shoulder.

Maybe if I knew more, I wouldn't have lied so much to my

friends when I was younger. It felt like Lucia's family had it all together. She knew about her abuelita's bisabuela. Where they came from. When they came to the States. They celebrated other holidays, and to bring in luck for the New Year, we'd eat twelve grapes—one for each month. And Christmas was always celebrated the night before, presents and everything.

There was this interconnectedness they had, and all Daddy could say was "You're Black, and you should be proud." And I was proud, but I wanted to know more. I felt like there was a hole carved in me without it. An intergenerational hole carved in all of us.

I pushed the blankets away from me as I tossed in bed, one foot hanging off the side.

Journeys end in lovers meeting.

Those words haunted me again. No time to remember the meaning of them or google the Shakespeare play. Now was time for sleep.

SIXTEEN

PAST: AUGUST, TWELVE YEARS AGO

Bubba tried to run away once. I was five, he was twelve.

I watched him, his cheeks red, as he stuffed his backpack with clothes, a phone charger, and crumpled-up dollar bills.

"Where you going?" I asked, and he ignored me. At first, I thought he couldn't hear me, and I repeated myself, but it only made him move faster.

I ran to his bed, trying to get to his backpack, but he was quicker, whipping it away and putting it on. *"Ugh!"* I squeezed my fingers into my palms. "Bubba, where are you going?!"

"Just go to bed, Hylee. Get out of my business." Bubba rushed out the back door into the summer night, clutching the straps of his backpack. He was already Mama's height, with long legs, and it was the only thing I could focus on as I hurried behind.

"Bubba. Wait. You can't leave." I coughed, the sticky air wrapping around my braids. I tried to plead with him, but he was halfway down the driveway now, the cicadas singing after him. *"Nooo,"* I cried once he passed the gate. "Please don't go. Don't leave me here."

He whipped around, snot leaking from his nose. His eyes puffy. I looked up at him—his dark curls swirled into the midnight sky. "I'm not going back in that house, Lee. You can't make me! Not with them!"

I didn't understand why he was so upset. "But you can't leave. I won't have anyone." My face stung when I said it, and he wiped his eyes with the back of his hand.

There was a hiccup with his next breath. "Mama and Daddy. They..." He shook his head. "You're just a baby, Lee. You wouldn't get it. Besides, you're better here than I am."

"But I'm not," I cried. "I'm not a baby."

"Go back inside."

"No." I stomped my foot, my eyes clearing.

He smacked his lips. "Just do it. Don't try to be grown."

I didn't move, and Bubba turned back around, walking down

the faded pavement. It was the first time I'd felt my heart break. The first time I'd realized that people you loved had the potential to take that love and set it on fire.

My limbs folded. I cried, feeling like my life had gone to ruins. Snot ran down my lips, and my face stung. It felt like the world was crumbling around me.

Bubba paused.

I watched his shoulders slump, and his head dropped. He shook it, mumbling something to the ground. The wind pushed the leaves in the tree, and that one—the one on the edge of the driveway—stretched its branches toward him.

Bubba came back. He turned around, his eyes shining when he placed a hand on my shoulder, and it was the only thing that stopped my tears. "Don't cry, Lee. It's okay."

I shook my head. It wasn't okay. Not when my very first friend was trying to leave the only home we knew.

He bent down to my eye level, and he took off his backpack. "I'm not gonna leave, okay?" He held up his hands, palms facing me.

"But you said you were."

"I know I did, but I changed my mind."

I didn't believe him. Even with his palms up, his bag on the ground. My bottom lip trembled. He could sneak off when I wasn't looking—he could be gone forever.

I just shook my head.

"Sissy, look. I pinkie promise, okay?" he said, and he held out his pinkie.

I sniffled. "Really?"

He nodded. "Really. And if I ever leave, I promise I'll bring you with me."

"You promise?"

"I *pinkie* promise."

I smiled, wiped at my face, and wrapped my pinkie around his. Then we walked back up the hill together, and I raced him to the back door, the tears drying on my face.

Bubba walked me to my room, and I refused to go in, my heels planted to the ground, my hands on the edge of the doorframe as he tried to push me past the threshold.

He rolled his eyes. "You get on my nerves. Always making things difficult." I smiled up at him, and I cheesed even harder when he asked if I wanted some Hot Chips.

We shared a bowl—even though he ate most of it—and we watched cartoons in the living room, my feet crisscrossed on the couch.

"That's you," I said, pointing to Squidward on the TV.

He laughed. "No it ain't!"

"Uh-huh!" I giggled until it turned into a squeal.

He shoved me, trying to knock me over, but I wouldn't budge. "It ain't. That's you! You got the big head, Lee!"

I threw a chip at him, but he caught it. "At least I have brains!" I said, and I stuck my tongue out.

He chuckled, changing the channel. "Nah, you just got a big ol' head."

"Yours is bigger!" And we bickered like that, laughing, as he flicked through the channels.

Our parents fought that night.

Loud, screaming. Something about money and how we didn't have much of it.

It was the first of many fights like that, but I didn't flinch because I had Bubba next to me. I wondered now if he ever regretted that promise, if he wished he could truly run away.

SEVENTEEN

PRESENT DAY: FEBRUARY

When I woke, the shirt I'd tied around my wet curls was crumpled on the floor.

Classic.

Grabbed my phone, my vision still foggy. No text from Lucia, but I needed to stop thinking that she'd respond. She wouldn't.

One message from Sarah, and two from Eilam. One was about ten minutes after I'd fallen asleep. The other one was about thirty minutes ago.

I'm glad you're alive

Good afternoon

The bold and rounded letters made me want to crawl into myself again because as I read those texts, I remembered how I disappeared in front of him. How there was no coming back from that.

But I also remembered his mouth fixed into a sly smile. How he smelled like something I knew. How I noticed more than I should have, and how that awareness made me feel unsettled.

Still, I didn't text him back. I didn't owe him anything. My life was so tangled, adding another person to it would only make it that much more complicated.

I rubbed my eyes and got dressed, remembering how I promised Sarah I'd hang out with her today. It was already noon. I pulled on Bubba's old Wu-Tang T-shirt and a pair of mom jeans before I stumbled into the bathroom to refresh my hair and pull it into a curly bun, leaving out just enough fringe to feel fearless.

Grandmommy was in the kitchen when I got downstairs. She was working on a thousand-piece puzzle set of different types of trees. It looked dreadful.

"Ah, I guess the caged bird does sing!" She said it without looking at me, and I crumpled my brows. "Good seeing you around."

I opened a cabinet, finding a glass to fill with water. "Oh, um. Long night."

"I noticed. Did anything happen?" Did she mean time travel? Disappear? Be swept into a totally different reality?

When I didn't say anything, she spoke again. "Hello, ma'am. I believe I asked you a question."

I took a big gulp of water, buying myself time.

She pursed her lips, returned her gaze to her puzzle. "Well, did you have fun at least?"

"Yeah. Loads."

Her colorful shawl moved as she picked up her coffee mug full of tea. It was all she ever drank these days. But I knew that she knew I was a lying liar. "If you're going to live here, Hylee, you need to be responsible, you hear? I don't want you running around the town thinking you can do this, that, and the other. You are my responsibility now."

I nodded my head, set the glass in the sink.

"You can verbally respond, you know."

"Sorry about that, Grandmommy. It won't happen again."

She mumbled something. "And can you please, for once, text me back? I know I'm old, but I'm not that old. *Please*." She smirked. "I lived through the seventies, child."

"Yeah, sorry about that. I'll do better."

Another mumble. Then a sigh. "Where are you off to?"

"I was hoping to hang out with Sarah. She lives down the street."

"Do I know Sarah?"

"No."

She picked up a puzzle piece, contemplated where to place it, and then dropped it. "That's fine. But text me when you get there."

I nodded my head.

"And clean that glass. I don't like stuff left in the sink."

I almost smacked my lips, but didn't. Daddy always told me he never got away with anything—that Grandmommy hovered over him like a shadow. But I did as she said, and as I was about to leave the kitchen, I paused. Turned around.

"Grandmommy," I said, taking a step forward. "What happened the night Bubba went missing?"

The afternoon sun shimmered in her dark brown hair, highlighting a few of the gray strands, and she didn't pause to look at me. She let her fingers brush over a few puzzle pieces before grabbing one. "I wasn't there that night."

"I know, but I was thinking maybe Mama or Daddy told you."

"Things were really mixed up that evening, unfortunately, baby. I don't know what else you want me to say."

I shrugged. The truth. I wanted the truth. "I just wish I knew what happened," I said, and even as I said it, I knew that blockage in my head wasn't being chipped away at all.

I saw flashes of that news article. Boy still missing. Break-in. Deadly shooting. Minor found hiding in tub.

Grandmommy glanced off somewhere. She was thinking, maybe remembering, and I waited a minute longer to see if she'd share, but nothing.

"Why won't any of you talk about it? You act like if you say his name, if you talk about that night, you'll be cursed."

"Please, honey. Don't push me."

"But, Grandmommy. Please. It's my history, too. Doesn't that matter? If I knew . . . I just want to know what's happening to me. Don't you? Don't you wish this wasn't happening and that life could be as it was? Don't you—"

Grandmommy scooted her chair away from the table, and the screeching startled me. Her hands rested on her thighs; her braid whipped across her shawl. Even before she spoke, her chest rose and fell quickly. "I am only going to say this once, and that's it." Her hazel eyes looked clear in the light, and she stared at me for a long time before she breathed another word. "We won't talk about it again after."

"Okay . . ." I took another step forward. Unsure what I was agreeing to.

"Here's the thing about reality: There's multiple truths."

I pulled my bottom lip in, confused.

"Listen. Reality...it doesn't exist in the way you think it does. Time's not linear, it's not how we've been taught. It's more than that, you hear? Time is only real because we *see* it that way. But at the end of the day, at the end of our lives, we choose to be who we want to be; just like how we choose to believe what we want to believe. And if we let ourselves believe it, we are infinite. We were always made to be infinite—our souls just got stuck in our bodies on the way down from the heavens. So for now, we're here, in my kitchen. But maybe in an alternate timeline, we're elsewhere."

Alternate timeline? Was she saying what I thought she was saying? Those words, they sounded like a riddle. Was there more to this that she wasn't sharing? "Are you saying that's what happened to me?"

Grandmommy didn't nod, she just stared.

Another step forward, my hands gripping the strap of my bag. "What else do you know?"

"Hylee." Her voice was cold like ice, her fingers gripping into her legs. A warning. She pulled herself back into the table, flipped her braid away from her shoulder, looked down at the puzzle. "We're not doing this today."

"But." And I stopped myself. She was done. She was done, and I knew that was all she would say. That she probably regretted saying anything. And what was I supposed to do? I wanted to stomp my feet, to yell and let the rising steam in my chest escape. They were all full of it, and I was so damn tired of everyone treating me like a child and keeping secrets from me like Bubba wasn't mine, too. Like the truth of that night didn't belong to me, too. But they did, and I would find out what happened. And the alternate timelines? What was I supposed to say in response to that? There had to be more.

I didn't yell. I didn't throw my bag on the ground like I wanted to. Instead, I said good-bye, grabbed a light sweater, and headed for the door, feeling Bubba's coin pressing into my back pocket.

The first thing I did when I was outside was clench my teeth. My jaw locked, and I had to take a moment to gather myself before I screamed or tried to kick something.

I ambled down the sidewalk, away from the cul-de-sac. I pulled my sketchbook out of my bag, creating a loose outline of my old house. Broken lines made windows that looked eerie and there wasn't a single cloud in sight, but every other blink brought darkness. Not like the darkness from behind my lids, but *darkness*. The kind that beckoned to me despite my desperate wishes to be left alone, to be normal.

I blinked twice as fast. One moment the houses were all beige-and-white siding and manicured green lawns; the next, ruins.

Vines twisting and crawling up the sides of them, choking away the color, making it dark gray. The roofs sagged and seeped like water had settled in the middle and sides of them, and the trees were long and thin and grew so tall they created shade around everything.

Then a cracking sound. Like someone was at the end of their wheezing, the end of their breath. My name then, low and smooth like silk. *Hylee.*

When my phone vibrated, the ruins were gone. The sound was gone.

It was Eilam.

So about last night

Can we talk?

Shit. No.

I paused on the sidewalk, chewing the inside of my lip so hard I tasted blood.

I didn't want to text him back. I wanted to pretend, let myself live on the idea that I'd met a boy yesterday, and everything was fine—and that we'd never see each other again, and that would also be fine. And, most importantly, that he'd never seen me disappear.

My phone was back in my pocket in a hurry, and I picked up the pace, trying to get to Sarah's house as fast as I could so I could have a distraction.

Sarah lived in a two-story, castlelike white house with big, curved windows, a long driveway, and evergreen trees that were shaped into spirals next to the pillars on the front porch.

The doorbell changed colors when I pressed it, and through the side windows, I could see narrow wooden floor boards, the end of a rug, and then a dog running to see who was here.

The golden retriever panted, saliva dripping from his tongue, and then the door swung open.

Sarah smiled. She had on loose, floral-printed pants and a black ribbed shirt that hugged her neck. "Hylee!" she sang, and then: "I hope you like dogs. Lucky is harmless, I promise," she said, pushing her short hair behind her ears as Lucky jumped up on his hind legs.

"Awww, I love dogs," I said, greeting Lucky as soon as I entered. His wet nose grazed mine, and he licked my cheek. I wiped my face and took off my shoes.

"I have the perfect chill afternoon planned for us."

I sighed in relief. "Like what?"

Sarah locked the front door, and then she started down the hall and up the circular staircase. "You'll see," she said, her lips twisting into a bright smile. I followed her, and the smell of pop-corn nestled in my nostrils with each step forward.

We turned a corner, and she pushed a door open that led to a big bedroom. Lucky rushed in ahead of us, stepping onto the pallet of blankets Sarah had spread across the floor of her room, looking like he had done it himself. There was an array of different-shaped pillows leaning against the end of her bed frame.

"Series Day!" she exclaimed as I stepped inside, noticing Netflix pulled up on her flat-screen TV. On her bedroom dresser, Sarah had lined up a few cans of bubbly water and assorted candy. There was also an overflowing blue bowl of popcorn, a bag of chips, and a plate of fresh-baked chocolate chip cookies.

My mouth watered, and I rolled onto the floor with a smile as Lucky rushed over to me.

This. Sarah didn't know how much I needed this. Normalcy and someone who didn't know any secrets about me. It reminded me of eighth-grade slumber parties with Lucia. We used to stay up till two in the morning, talking about our crushes, binge-watching reality TV, and spending hours and hours stalking our friends on social media. All that was over now, but I tried not to think about it too much.

Lucky licked my cheek, and my phone vibrated. Damn it. There was no way that could be Eilam. So what if he saw me disappear?

He didn't need to keep texting me to remind me of my own impending doom.

"How's your weekend been so far?" Sarah sat on the floor with me, the remote in her hands, and I sat up, pushing my hands down Lucky's fur and trying to will myself into forgetting about the text that I refused to check.

I sucked my lips in first, and then I let out a breath so big my shoulders dropped. "Last night I got drunk for the first time."

When I said it, Sarah turned her entire body toward me, dropping the remote and then resting her chin on the back of her hand with stars in her eyes. "You have my full attention."

I chuckled, covering my face before telling her the entire story, minus the part where I was sucked out of the universe and dropped into a disturbing version of reality featuring my childhood home.

I didn't tell her about the ruins I'd seen on my way here. Didn't say a word about the constant voice in my head, or the hands I kept seeing. But still...I was honest, for once. I told her about Eilam, about the music and the people. I told her about me throwing up and sneaking back inside Grandmommy's house, and I told her about the headache I had now.

Sarah left and returned with ibuprofen, and I grabbed a can of bubbly before I popped two in my mouth and drank the soda water.

"I've gotten pretty wasted before," Sarah admitted. She was sitting up straighter now, her legs stretched. "You'll probably think it's silly, but for my brother's eighteenth birthday, my parents rented him a yacht. Yeah, you don't have to say it. I already know what you're thinking: *You're rich!*" she said, her voice whiney.

"I was definitely thinking it."

"Most people do. But anyway, my parents had a full bar there, and me and my friends would sneak around them once they'd set their drinks down, and we'd finish whatever was in their cup without them knowing. The idea was genius until we'd gotten so drunk, it was hard to stand up straight. That was the night I learned that you apparently aren't supposed to mix liquor."

I made a face. "That sounds like the worst possible scenario. *Annnd* being on a boat, too."

"Right. Whenever I look at a boat now, my stomach turns."

"You have to admit, though, it sounds like it was fun."

She smiled. "It was." Sarah grabbed the remote and clicked through several titles before selecting one. She dimmed the lights and pressed play, and I grabbed one of the blankets and wrapped it around myself as Lucky pushed between the two of us.

Only a few minutes into the movie, I remembered the text notification I'd received earlier. I slipped my fingers into my pocket, pulling out my phone and unlocking it.

It was exactly who I thought it was: Eilam.

I'd like to meet up with you tonight

I'll be working at post coffee shop until 9

EIGHTEEN

The moon had a thick bleeding ring around it by the time Sarah and I had finished our movie marathon, and I was curled up in my sweater when Sarah agreed to drop me off at the coffee shop that Eilam worked at. I'd given in because I couldn't stop thinking about it. My stomach knotted, and I just wanted to get this over with.

It was strange knowing that he'd invited me to a place where he *worked*. It felt like a boundary being crossed, and to be completely frank, I wasn't sure if it was the right place to meet, because this conversation would be confrontational. It had to be. Why else text so many times?

Sarah pulled into a parking spot in front of a building with gray paneling that sat on the end of an old strip mall. Most of the windows were replaced with garage doors, and a few of them were open, allowing me to see directly inside the building.

Inside there were painted white walls with light brown floating shelves that held fat, leafy plants. Concrete floors and industrial lighting. Scattered tables and chairs. A couple sitting at a table, their feet touching as they stared into each other's eyes. A man over there, facing toward the window, with headphones on and a laptop out. And a small group of people by the couch. They all had matching books.

I thanked Sarah as I got out of the car, and I squeezed the straps of my crossbody bag as I entered the building. A woman with curly blond hair greeted me while wiping down a table, and the smell of espresso made me want to hold a warm cup of it to my nose.

Right there, behind the L-shaped bar, I saw Eilam. His warm pecan skin was a contrast to everything else in the building, a smile twisting in the corner of his lips. That same smile from last night. He wore a baggy beanie that covered his curls, and he held a hand up, motioning me to come over.

It bugged me that he didn't seem nervous or afraid that the

disappearing act was on her way to see him. Unless…unless I imagined everything. Unless Lucia was right, and none of it had happened at all.

But then, why did Eilam want to see me so bad?

"Order whatever you want. It's on me," he said, and I felt this incomprehensible strangeness. There was something about his presence that made me feel like we were longtime friends, like I'd come to this coffee shop and ordered pastries and lattes time and time again.

I cleared my throat, not looking him directly in the eyes, because I couldn't anymore. Not after he saw me vanish. "I'll take an Americano with almond milk and vanilla."

"Sure thing. My shift ends in a couple of minutes. I'll meet you on the patio." Something in his voice when he said it. Intrigue, tenderness—none of which I expected.

I didn't say *okay*, but I thought it. Still couldn't bring myself to look at him. If I didn't see his eyes, didn't see his face, it might hurt less when this—whatever this was between us—was over. Then, if he really saw me vanish last night, I wouldn't have to remember the look in his eyes.

When I entered the cool night again, I could smell the edge of rain entering the air. A storm coming soon, which made sense. The clouds were moving quickly past the stars.

I wrapped my arms around myself tightly, sat in a chair at a wooden table that faced one of the windows. I could leave now if I wanted. And maybe Eilam had us sit out here because he knew I'd need an easy out. The walk back home would be long, but it would be better than whatever was about to unfold.

My phone vibrated.

Please don't forget to be home before ten.

Right. Grandmommy probably didn't want a repeat of Friday. I texted her back, letting her know I'd be home soon.

After I sent it, I found myself looking over my shoulder multiple times, waiting for Eilam to arrive with fear in his eyes and shaky breath.

Or maybe he'd record me on his phone, get evidence to show the world how strange this all was.

Or maybe he'd freeze like how Lucia had when she saw it the first time. Maybe we'd sit across from each other not saying a thing.

My feet bounced as I tried to hold everything together. I wanted to channel Sarah—her confidence and grace was inspiring, and I needed a shot of that to get me through this meeting with Eilam.

A whoosh of air made my bangs move. Distant chatter, light music, and then: "An Americano with almond milk and vanilla." Eilam placed the drink in front of me. "An espresso for me," he said, and he pulled out the chair across from me, the metal scraping the concrete.

When he sat down, I felt my breathing stutter. He took a sip of espresso, his bony hands raising the mug to his face.

There was a small smile tucked at the side when he set his drink down. I didn't get why he was smiling, or if he was just playing nice, but for whatever reason, it made me blush a little.

"Why do you seem so cool about everything?" I blurted out.

He coughed, his espresso going down too fast. "I guess we're bypassing the small talk, then."

I leaned back, my hands in my lap as I squeezed them together, my heart racing. "Don't you have burning questions?"

He set his tiny white mug down. "I do."

"So, are you gonna ask me, or . . . ?"

"Or?" he repeated, shifting in his seat to get more comfortable.

"It's a rhetorical *or*."

"Right," he said, grinning again. "Are you gonna try the Americano?"

I stared down at my drink, a velvety smooth brown with fluffy white froth creeping around the edges. It looked good, but it smelled even better. I looked him in the eyes. "Depends. Did you poison it?"

Eilam laughed. "You can't be serious."

I didn't respond because I was, in fact, very serious. Plus, it wasn't like it was an outrageous question to ask. I didn't know what his intentions were.

Eilam took another sip before he said anything else. Then he sat back again, his shoulders relaxed, his body leaning to the side. "I didn't poison your drink because I don't want to kill you."

That seemed true. He wouldn't invite me to his job to feed me poison. It was an irrational thought. I sighed, and then I picked up the mug, looked him in the eye. He had to see this. Held his gaze and took a sip. *There.*

Eilam folded his lips, tried to hide a smile. What was with that? It was the way his smile *was*, how it emerged in this space, making me want to smile too, but I held my guard. Even if something inside me felt like I'd smiled for him hundreds of times before, I couldn't trust anyone, least of all myself.

"So . . . what did you see last night?"

He leaned in. "We're really diving right in, huh?"

Did I need to answer that again? He wanted me here, so unless he had another motive, I was going to dive in headfirst. And if he saw what I thought he did, I needed to know so I could protect myself.

I couldn't pinpoint what to expect with an outsider knowing my secret, but anything could happen. For all I knew, this invitation could be his way of letting me down easy because maybe he called a scientist so they could poke and prod at me, so they could figure out why I kept disappearing for their own personal gain. And maybe they were on their way. And maybe this was his way of stalling until they got here.

When I went to speak, he cut me off. "You want to know everything?"

I nodded. *And don't leave a single detail out,* I wanted to say. But I gulped, trying to keep my drink from coming back up.

And he . . . you know what he did? He leaned forward, locking eyes with me because he wanted me to know that everything he was about to say was the truth. And he wanted to watch me, to maybe see how I'd break at the sound of it.

"We were sitting on the hood of my car, talking. I was on the left side, and you were on the right." He paused. Was that important? "You seemed a little disoriented, but I figured it must have been from whatever you'd drank. I asked for your number because it looked like you might pass out, and I wanted to make sure you got home safely. That was important to me." He paused again. No break in his stare. "Then you gripped my jacket. You mumbled something, but I wasn't sure what it was you said because the words rushed out, and then you were gone. You disappeared in front of me." His jaw clenched, and it wasn't the right time, but I . . . I liked the way it looked. The way his muscles tightened beneath his skin.

A swallow. He sat up straighter. "It felt like I'd imagined it at first, like it was me. But then I tried looking for you. I went back to the party, asked a few people if you came inside to grab something, but you were gone. I went back to my car, looking for any sign of you. Proof that you were here, and I remembered I had your number, so I called and texted you, hoping that you'd respond. You didn't—not until later—and that's what happened," he said definitely. His eyes dropped. "That's everything."

I didn't move at first, didn't even breathe. It was true; he'd seen me disappear. And it was real. It was *real*, because why would this stranger lie to me? This guy who didn't owe me anything, who knew nothing about me except my name, and the fact that I could disappear into thin air.

"You saw me disappear." It wasn't loud when I said it, and I didn't think I'd voiced it until he responded.

"Yes . . . I saw you disappear." The words came slowly when he repeated them back to me, still so foreign.

"Why are you so nonchalant about it?"

"*Nonchalant* is an understatement to how I feel. Honestly, I freaked out a lot. But the thing about a word is . . . you kept yours. You said you'd meet me here tonight, and well, here we are."

I took a sip of my Americano. He didn't know that I had almost stood him up, that even as he made my drink, I'd considered walking away. A different kind of disappearance. One I could control for once. "And that was enough for you?"

A slow nod, and then that damn smile again, forming as he

twisted his cup on the table. "Yup. Though it wasn't like I had many options. You get that, right?"

"I feel like most people would have called the police or reported me to some science society or something."

"Maybe I'm not most people."

I pursed my lips. Rolled my eyes. I couldn't handle the whole I'm-not-like-most-people thing. Not right now.

He dropped his hands below the table. "But what would I have said?" he pressed, then pretended to hold a phone to his ear. *"Hey, police? Yeah, this girl I just met disappeared in front of me. Yup. Uh-huh. Send everyone.* Come on. They'd probably think I was joking."

I shrugged. It wasn't my problem what the police would have thought. The fact was this: Those who saw me disappear freaked out. My family, my mom's friend, and especially Lucia. So even if Eilam wasn't "most people," I didn't buy it. Maybe he wanted something.

"Can I ask you something? What happened to you after you disappeared?"

Took another sip. The drink almost gone now, and when I swallowed, all I could see was the little girl's face in my head again. I heard her scared, labored breathing in my ear. So, so close. And I could still feel her small, cold hands covering my mouth before I screamed.

He wouldn't believe me if I told him, and frankly, I still didn't trust him. Sure, he didn't report me anywhere, but the way he stared at me made me believe that he was taking notes so he could write a documentary on me and cash in on it later. Maybe I was vain to think that, but he was still a stranger.

"C'mon. *Try me*," he said when I didn't say anything.

Released a deep breath. "You wouldn't believe me if I told you."

"But I already believe you." He repositioned himself, leaning in almost. "How's it that I got more out of you last night in a few minutes than in this whole coffee date?"

I leaned in, too. "Have you considered that time changes things?"

"I know for a fact that time changes things."

I squinted, hating how sure he sounded. "Look, the moment I tell you, you're gonna think I'm—"

"What? A little off?"

I crossed my arms, and he smiled. "Don't mock me."

"It's not like that, I promise." Then he lowered his voice. "I saw what happened to you, Hylee. I'm not here to judge you." His voice was normal again. "I'm genuinely curious."

I pressed my fingers together, and I looked at them while I spoke. "I ended up in the past, and it's hard to explain, but the reality there isn't . . . it's not like the reality here."

Eilam's brows were low when I looked up. "What do you mean?"

"I mean it's dark there. Always dark. Even the colors seem

muted somehow. But even stranger . . . the *girl* that I've seen. She looks like a monster." I chewed my lip and waited. There. It was said. But he didn't take out some secret recording device. Didn't push himself away from the table, disgust in his eyes. Instead, he cocked his head to the side, thinking.

"A monster? But . . . how do you know it's the past?"

"Yeah, at least, I think. And it's the past because I was taken to my childhood home. I haven't lived there in almost a decade, but all my things were there, exactly how I left them. That would be impossible today. I know no one lives there."

He raised a brow. "You know that for a fact?"

"Well . . . no." My voice lowered. "It's more of a guess."

He shifted—it looked like he had so many thoughts running through his head at once, an expression that was impossibly, inexplicably familiar. Almost annoyingly so. "Maybe it's a different version of the past?"

"That's if we're even saying that time travel is real."

"It is real. You're living proof of that, aren't you? Plus, Einstein never said time travel *wasn't* real."

"What do you know about Einstein?"

"I know he coined the term *relativity*, which essentially says that time and space are linked together. The faster you travel, the slower you experience time. And nothing can travel faster than the speed of light." He paused. "But, well, then there's you—"

"An anomaly," I finished.

He lifted a finger. "Nah, I didn't say all that. But you're certainly breaking the rules of time somehow, and from your story, you're also breaking the rules of the universe, because if you went back to the past—a *different* past, then that's . . ."

"An alternate universe."

"Exactly," he said, smiling at me. And it was the thing Grandmommy said earlier that haunted me. *Time isn't as it seems.* What else did she know, and why was she being so secretive? If anything, she should be sharing everything in hopes that it would help ease the madness.

I was hesitant to ask, but . . . "Do you know anything about that?"

"I know two things. Some white dude who did research in quantum theory once said his equations described several different histories that weren't alternate histories, but histories that happened *simultaneously*."

I scoffed. "How do you know this?"

"I spent a lot of time inside as a kid."

"I mean, we're *still* kids."

"Speak for yourself."

"Wait. How old are you?"

"Seventeen. You?"

I rolled my eyes. "We're the same age. Anyway, you said you know two things. If that's the first, then what's the second?"

"Right. So, going back to all my free time indoors, I read a lot of comics. Time travel, alternate universes—that's normal in these stories."

He was right. I hadn't read any comics, but I'd seen movies, TV shows. They were all there, but I hadn't realized the connection until now.

"There's one last thing, actually. Astronomers and cosmologists have been studying the multiverse recently. The multiverse is the idea that each alternate universe carries its own version of reality. There's this version of reality—the one where you and I are talking on the patio at my job—and there's maybe another one, where you and I are mortal enemies."

"Enemies? Why enemies?"

"It's just an example, but . . . if you're down for it, I have other theories."

"Eilam," I said, and he looked so sincere when he held my gaze. "You seem nice and all, but I don't know why I should trust you."

"Then why are you here?"

I wanted to back away from the table. "Because," I started, and I swallowed hard, anxious. And in the evening, behind him, lingering against the side of the building, I thought I saw the silhouette of a girl. No eyes. She had no eyes, and her pigtails stretched into dark fingers, twisting in the breeze.

It made me freeze at first, and then I spoke quickly, my words almost tripping over themselves. "Because I don't want this to get out. I'm not going around telling people about this, okay? No one should know. *You* shouldn't know," I clarified. "And I don't want you telling anyone."

He clenched his jaw again, looked away for a second, and I wondered if I'd offended him. It wasn't intentional, but I couldn't lie about this part.

We were silent for too long, and I was nervous that the shadows behind him would stretch and consume us.

Eilam sat up taller. This, whatever it was he was going to say, he meant it. "I'm not . . . I'm not going to tell anyone, and maybe you can't trust me now, but give me a chance to earn it." Eilam twisted his lips. He wanted to earn my trust. *Earn.* "What if I told you I had a big secret, too?"

NINETEEN

Truth was, I didn't want Eilam to feel like he needed to share a secret with me.

The thought that he had a big secret (assuming no one else knew) was magnetizing, but the realization that he still knew about my own secret didn't make me feel comfortable in the slightest.

And he wouldn't stop looking at me.

It was like he was waiting for something. The second he opened his mouth to speak, his phone started vibrating uncontrollably.

and he held his finger up, stepped away from the table, and disappeared around the building.

I could feel the bumps in my spine as I pressed my back against the chair, trying my best to hear what conversation was taking place over the light breeze and the whooshing from cars passing by.

Was that a chuckle I heard? Maybe it was his girlfriend. Boys like Eilam weren't single, and if they were, they usually weren't into me. Wasn't sure why that was, but I'd had enough rejection to know that the guys I liked had a certain type, and whatever that was, it wasn't me.

I tapped my foot, trying to hear more and settle the bubbles in my stomach. If he was dating someone, why'd he look at me like that? If a stare was a single story, he was giving me an entire book. I wanted to highlight his paragraphs and fold his corners so I wouldn't forget my place.

He came back around the corner, his brown cheeks flushed with a tint of red. It probably was his girlfriend, then. Guess I should throw the whole book away.

"Hey, sorry about getting up like that. I actually have a family emergency." He started to grab his empty espresso mug, then stopped, noticing I hadn't moved. "Do you have a ride home?"

No. I didn't. I hated that I didn't. Embarrassed because of it. If Lucia were here, she'd say, *See, that's why planning is so important.* I hated and loved her for it. I couldn't estimate time for shit, and admittedly, her pestering had made me somewhat better, not that you could tell judging by how today was going.

"I don't," I said, my voice low.

He tilted his head toward the coffee shop door. "Can I give you a ride home?"

I nodded, getting up and following him inside. We placed our items in a dirty dish bin, and then I waited while Eilam grabbed his things from the break room.

Outside, he opened the passenger door to his Pontiac, and I slid into the seat and prayed my stomach wouldn't make any awful whale sounds while we were in the car together. But my hands were already shaky from the coffee, my stomach tossing and turning.

He plugged my address into the maps app on his phone and then backed out of the parking spot. "Is everything okay? I asked, and he looked confused at first. "You said you had a family emergency."

"Everything's okay. I guess it sounds bigger than it is, but I just have to pick up my little brother from his stepmom's. I hope you're okay with me doing that before I drop you off."

I nodded and he flipped through the radio stations, like there could possibly be anything good on the radio. Then, a smile.

"What was that?"

He tried to hide his face, looking behind him now to see if a car was coming. "What was *what*?"

"*That*," I repeated, trying to get him to look at me. "You're all smiley."

"You want to know?" he asked, glancing my way, and I just stared at him blankly. "The last time we were together, you said you wouldn't get in a car with me. I find the irony funny."

Together. He'd said it like we had planned to hang out yesterday. He'd said it with hope, and it made me smile. "I did say that, didn't I?"

"Loud and clear." He pulled onto another road, and then we were silent, and in the silence, I noticed how dark and small the car was, and how it smelled like evergreens and old leather. How the warm air pushing through the vents wasn't warm enough to stop the chills in my arms. How the seat squeaked each time I moved.

"Did you know it was about to happen?" he asked, and I was surprised we were talking about it again. We were at a stoplight, and the red light highlighted his cheekbones, painted the stubble around his mouth, glistened in his brown eyes. At least he was listening, interested. It made me feel less alone.

"Not until it was too late," I admitted. The light turned green then, and I couldn't see Eilam's face as we turned onto a road lined with bright headlights and the sound of impatient engines.

"Did it hurt at all?"

"It makes me nauseous, and it sends tingling through my blood right as it happens. Kind of like my muscles are falling asleep."

We were in a neighborhood now. It wasn't a new development like where Grandmommy lived, but it was still nice. Older, two-level homes with enough space in between them. Fresh sidewalks, bright white streetlights.

"And that's when you ended up in an alternate reality," he said, putting the pieces of my story together as he pulled into a driveway of a home with big windows and small lights illuminating the path to the front door.

"If *that's* what we're calling it," I murmured.

"It is. I'm confident of that."

I wanted to challenge him. I hated how he spoke so definitively. He didn't really know.

But I didn't say anything, because the car was in park when he said it, and then he turned off the engine. A long pause, then a deep breath. "Okay, um. I have to go in there and grab my little brother." He said it like he was nervous I'd get out and leave. I thought about it, but I wasn't going to do it. "I'll be right back."

Eilam entered the night, leaving the smell of coffee behind him.

He knocked on a fancy black door to a fancy white house with black shutters. He was inside for maybe a minute. Probably even less than that, and when he reappeared, he jogged toward the car with a car seat in hand.

My brows crumpled when he opened the back door. How *little* was this brother?

"Just gotta put this in first," he said, his words all breathy as he climbed into his backseat and connected a car seat in the middle. Then he was gone again, back inside the house that had swallowed him earlier.

I tapped my thumb on my knee while I waited, and when Eilam returned, he wore a Spider-Man backpack, and curled around his hip was a toddler with dinosaur-print footie pajamas.

The kid waved to the floating brown hand in the doorway, and his excitement radiated off him as he swung his feet and flashed his small teeth.

The boy had brown skin and tight, curly hair that spiraled in all directions. He had a small button nose, a little dimple beneath his eye, and he was almost identical to Eilam, crooked smile and all.

He pointed to the car as Eilam said something to him, and my heart thumped in my chest. I wondered what he was saying. Was Eilam telling him about me?

The back door opened, and I braced myself. The opening swept in the cool night air and the sound of tiny chuckles. Then clips buckling and Eilam whispering something he didn't want me to hear.

"Hi," a small, giggling voice said. "Who are you?"

"Remember?" Eilam cut in. "Her name is *Hylee*."

"Oh," he said.

"Oh," Eilam mocked, and I turned to look at them. "This is my little brother, Julius." He said it right before he shut the door and returned to his spot in the driver's seat.

"Hi, Julius." I smiled at him, and he smiled back.

"Hi. Are we gonna go home now and play a game?" he asked, his little feet kicking.

"Sorry, Bubs. Hylee isn't hanging out with us tonight. She's going to her own home."

An aching squeeze, deep down in my soul. *Bubs.* That's what he called his little brother. It sounded so much like Bubba, and this feeling, the one that lingered in the car now, made me wish this ability I had let me travel back in time to when my brother was still here. Not the alternate reality bullshit, but *this* reality. The one where we were living and breathing in the same space before he disappeared.

There were people I knew who hated their brothers, but I couldn't fathom that. My brother used to be my everything. Not just my blood, but I wanted to mimic him like how mimes mimicked emotions. We were sworn partners in crime, through and through. And that's what I felt here, in this car, between Eilam and Julius. Brothers, best friends.

"Aw, man," Julius said, disappointed. I stared at Eilam. I just stared—at the profile of his face. The way his nose dipped at the tip, and how his cheeks rose as he laughed.

Only ten minutes until we'd be at Grandmommy's, but time would not move for me. And there was this sudden gravitational pull between both our bodies—like the solar system stopped spinning for a single second. It was Eilam and this moment. Eilam in the darkness with his teeth flashing in the night as he spoke to his brother, and I . . . I felt this force so vivid and wild inside me, like every cell in my body was yelling at me, saying, *You're supposed to be here. You're supposed to be here.*

Then Eilam looked over at me before making a turn, short and quick. A double take. A smile in the corner of his lips, and then the sound came rushing in. "Maybe next time," he said, but it wasn't to me, it was to Julius. Still, his voice gave me butterflies.

I turned to see Julius. I knew what to say to him. "Maybe, if your brother thinks I'm cool enough, we can *all* hang out together."

Julius's jaw dropped, his hands squeezing in fists before him, and Eilam made a sound. Somewhere between a scoff and a laugh. I'd surprised him.

"Woah. Do you think she's cool enough to hang out with us?"

Eilam rubbed his chin with his finger, sneaking a glance in the rearview mirror. "Hmm, I don't know, Bubs. It's hard to tell with this one."

"Oh." Julius paused. His shoulders dropped. "Maybe next time she can come over and we can play Smash?"

Eilam laughed and looked at me. But it was a different kind of look. "Yeah, maybe she can come over next time, and we can all play Smash. But it's up to Hylee."

"Oh, okay," Julius said. "It's up to Lee," he repeated, trying to say my name. My brother used to call me that. *Lee.* No one said it around me anymore, so afraid that I'd crumble into tiny particles at the whisper of it.

"That's right. We never want to assume anything, ever."

"Okay," Julius said again. "Maybe she can come over tomorrow and we can play Smash."

Eilam and I laughed, and I was unsure how well Julius understood the concept of time. Julius laughed, too, his small voice squealing over ours.

Only a few minutes away from Grandmommy's house now, and the laughs slowed down, but didn't stop completely.

Turned out, Julius was curious by nature. He asked a lot of questions. It wasn't for any real reason, at least not one that I knew, other than he just liked to talk. A lot.

So we talked, and we laughed, and a part of me hoped that somewhere in between the breaths of air, Eilam would somehow forget about me time traveling, and I could snap my fingers and pretend that none of the weird shit that was happening to me was happening to me, and that I could be an ordinary girl in a world that was very much like this one.

We pulled into the driveway, and Julius asked, "Is Lee leaving now?"

Eilam and I looked at each other. Long, deep, shared sighs, a moment that was both foreign and familiar. And he said, "Yeah, Bubs, Hylee has to go now." But he didn't look like he wanted me to go. His stare all wide and wanting.

I'd be remiss if I lied to myself and said I didn't feel the same. Because this was how it began. All big eyes and thumping heart-beats. But, I reminded myself, I didn't trust him. I didn't *know* him.

I broke away to grin in the shadows, and Julius said, "Oh, okay." Grinned again. That had been his response to everything: *"Oh."*

After I grabbed my bag, my hand lingered on the handle. "It was nice meeting you, Julius," I said over my shoulder.

"Tomorrow can you come over and we can play?"

"Bubs, Hylee can't come over tomorrow because we have plans, okay?"

"Okay."

"But maybe sometime soon," I promised, opening the door and climbing out. "Bye," I said to both of them, and they waved at me, Julius yelling, "Byeee!" and Eilam just grinning as I shut the door.

When I stepped away from the car, I saw Eilam grab his phone, his thumbs moving quickly. I hurried away then, but I felt my phone vibrate in my pocket. It was Eilam.

> Maybe you can come over and we can play smash sometime soon? :)

He was smiling at me when I turned around, and he backed out of the driveway. I waited in the darkness and watched him pull away, secretly wishing that it wasn't over yet. That I was still in that car. The warm air from the vents on my face. Half-heartedly laughing at a toddler and waiting for Eilam to sneak a glance at me.

The lights were dimmed inside the house, the smell of candles burning, and the sound of some news broadcaster over-enunciating a horrific event that happened this weekend.

Grandmommy was in the kitchen, a steaming cup of tea beside her as she continued to work on her puzzle. It was as if she hadn't moved all day.

"Hylee," she said at the sight of me, her voice urgent, and she stood. "Did you see my last text?" She looked at the time and back at me. "Are you okay? Is everything all right? You were supposed to be here at ten."

It was twenty past the hour, and I sighed. I should have said something. Given her a heads-up. "Grandmommy, I'm sorry," I said, and I really was. I was still getting used to being "checked up" on. My parents had given me more independence than I asked for.

"You know it's one of the—"

"Rules. I know, and I'm really sorry, and it won't happen again."

Her chest sank a little, and she sat back down. "Let's hope not," she mumbled. I felt bad, but also confused. Bad because I needed to be a better person, and I felt like I was breaking Grandmommy's trust every chance I got.

And confused because I still remembered what she'd said earlier today. About the multiple truths and the fluidity of time, and no way she could sit there and pretend like she didn't say any of that. No way could she actually be upset with me when we both knew she was holding out.

I grabbed a mug for tea, and the voice inside me crawled down my spine as I moved. *Hylee*, it said. *Hylee*. Was it the dark place calling to me before it swept me away, or was it just that the sound of that voice had stained my thoughts?

When the tea bag was in the cup, the water steaming and rising to my nose, I paused. Turned to look at Grandmommy as she picked up a puzzle piece. "I know you said you don't know what happened the night my brother disappeared, but... I'm gonna keep asking," I said, because everything I did was so that I wouldn't forget what I wanted to remember—him. Bubba.

Even if he had nothing to do with what was happening to me, why I was time traveling, then maybe that night did. Because why else would I be taken to that day if there weren't secrets left unresolved?

Grandmommy didn't say anything, so I kicked off my shoes, placed them in the washroom, and headed upstairs. I washed my face and brushed my teeth, trying my best not to pick at the scab on my chin from a pimple I popped the other day. After I put my hair in two braids and showered, I pulled on an oversized gray shirt and a pair of spandex shorts before sitting at my desk.

The warm light from the lamp brightened the wood and the empty page before me.

I put my pencil down and picked my phone up. Scrolled to the next screen, opened Spotify, pressed play. Still no texts from Lucia. I responded to Eilam.

Maybe

It was all I said.

He liked it immediately, and I smiled, picking up my pencil and beginning a new sketch. I drew until my thoughts were emptied and all that was left were the lyrics bleeding out of the speaker on my phone.

If I love you *was a promise,*

Would you break it, if you're honest?

TWENTY

PAST: SEPTEMBER, TEN YEARS AGO

Daddy said it was too early to go to my friend's house up the street, and Bubba was watching something on YouTube. He said he'd play with me later.

I poked my lip out. His loss.

My feet were bare as I ran across the black asphalt of our driveway to the gazebo that sat at the opening of our backyard.

I giggled the whole way there, my stomach tight because if Mama knew I was out here without shoes on... Shoot. She'd be so mad she'd make me help her with dishes for a week. She'd probably make me take out the trash, too, but that was Bubba's job. Ain't nobody got time to be taking out trash.

The gazebo was made of wood, and if you looked hard enough, you could see the flowers I carved into the corners with an old pen I found lying around in the basement.

I sighed, smiled, and put on an old apron Mama left out here for me. The gazebo was my house, and the best part about it was that I could do whatever I wanted. Today, I was Princess Tiana, and I owned my own restaurant. But first, I needed ingredients.

I grabbed a bowl from a small plastic bin underneath the patio set, and I rushed into the backyard singing and collecting leaves from the trees. The yellow daisies and white dandelions were too pretty to pass up. A few strands of grass for a little razzle-dazzle, and small brown sticks for mixing and cutting.

In the middle of tossing a salad, all I could think about was a nice cup of red Kool-Aid. Daddy had made some last night, and he'd let me take a small sip of it before I went to bed, but he said I couldn't have any until dinner tonight, but it was all I wanted now. Just a small sip. Mama and Daddy didn't have to know, and Bubba wouldn't care. Maybe he'd have a sip with me.

When I took off my apron, a car pulled into the driveway from the back end. It was green, and I'd never seen it before, so I ducked into the gazebo, peering out through the small openings.

A white lady with short, messy hair got out, looked back like she saw me, and then hurried up the porch steps to the back door.

Didn't remember seeing her ever, and I swallowed hard. Did Bubba know someone was coming over?

I crept to the side of the house. The driveway was hot on my bare feet, the sun overhead blinding me and making everything too bright. I ran up the rest of the driveway and cracked open the front door. Bubba wasn't in the living room, but the TV was still on, playing some YouTube video of a guy streaming *COD*.

Daddy's voice was the first thing I heard, and it was low, but I heard him say something to Bubba. I tiptoed to the hallway, so I could peek into the kitchen, and I could see the back of Daddy's head. He was talking to that lady.

She was almost as tall as Daddy, and I couldn't stop looking at her face 'cause she had on big glasses, and her cheeks looked real skinny, but they had these big holes in them. Like someone took a spoon to her face and scooped away small pieces.

Then Daddy moved away from her, and I ducked again, only returning when I heard him tell Bubba to "get that." And I looked again. Bubba came out of nowhere, his shoulders all droopy when he took a wad of money from the lady with the wild hair.

Then Daddy came back, a small plastic baggie in his hand, and he gave it to her, and she smiled, and Bubba turned around, and he saw me.

He saw me and his eyes were all big. And he shook his head and ran over to me, and I wished I could have just crawled into the corner and pretended I wasn't right there.

I didn't know what it was Daddy gave her, but she paid for it, and it made me feel all sick inside. I just knew that I never wanted to see her again, and I wished I wasn't here.

I wished I could disappear.

Bubba pulled me into the basement with him, and he flipped on the light to the steps and closed the door behind him.

His face looked puffy. "Lee, how long were you right there?"

I didn't say anything. I just felt my ears get hot.

"Did you see everything?"

I nodded, my eyes welling, and I tried to tell him that I just wanted some Kool-Aid, but my mouth started to shake when I tried to speak.

Bubba wrapped me in his arms, and I cried. I didn't know why, just that I felt scared. For him. For Daddy. For me.

Bubba kissed my head, and he pulled away and looked me straight in my eyes. "It's gonna be okay, Lee," he said, and he wiped the tears away from my cheek. "I'm gonna make sure Daddy never does this again, okay?"

I nodded and I was so thirsty still. "What was that? What Daddy had, and who was that white lady?"

He shook his head. "It was something that should have never

happened. Ever. And it's not gonna happen again. I promise." He held his pinkie out, and I didn't want to take it.

"But..." And my voice was loud, but Bubba shook his head, put a finger to his mouth.

"You weren't supposed to see that."

And I felt mad.

I felt like he was leaving me out, and I wasn't just a kid. I wanted to know things.

"Daddy doesn't want you to know about this."

"But that's not fair. You know, and everyone knows but me."

"It's not a good thing, Lee. Mama doesn't know. Daddy doesn't want her to know, so you can't tell her. You gotta promise you won't say anything."

"But *who* is she?"

"It doesn't matter who she is, but she's never coming back."

I started to cry again, and Bubba looked behind him, at the door that led to the hallway, and he tried to shush me. "Lee, come on. Please. It's adult things."

"But you're not an adult. You're just a teenager."

Bubba smacked his lips, and he sighed. "If I tell you this one thing, will you please stop crying?"

I nodded.

"And will you promise to keep the secret?"

I nodded again.

"Daddy got fired. He lost his job, and he's been trying to make money on the side while he finds a new one. And Mama can't know 'cause she always gets stressed out. But we're gonna be okay, and Daddy said he thinks he has something lined up, and it doesn't matter because I'm gonna do what I can to make sure Daddy doesn't do anything stupid, but you can't tell anyone, okay?"

I just. I swallowed so hard. "Okay."

"I promise, Lee. Everything's gonna be okay, and I'm always gonna protect you. I pinkie promise." Bubba held his pinkie out again, and I locked it with mine.

"Wanna go up to the school and play tetherball?"

I nodded my head, still shaken up from what Bubba said.

I didn't know Daddy could lie to Mama. And that Bubba could lie, too. And now I had to lie because Daddy got fired, and now he was getting money from a strange lady after giving her stuff. And what was it, anyway?

"Stay down here. I'm gonna check to make sure the coast is clear and then we can go."

I didn't say anything, and I didn't move as Bubba opened the door and disappeared on the other side. It felt like forever before he came back for me, and my stomach and my chest hurt, and I wondered what it meant to be broke.

TWENTY-ONE

PRESENT DAY: FEBRUARY

I woke to a song stuck in my head, and the sound of something scraping against paper in long strokes.

Swish, swish, swish.

My right hand gripped something so tight I felt my nails digging into my skin. The sound louder—the *swish, swish, swish* terrifying me—forcing my vision to come quicker.

Flinching eyes, and then I saw.

I saw I was sitting at my desk in my new room at Grandmommy's house. My back hunched over, the shining of the lamp glorifying what was before me.

What made me almost cry was that my right arm kept moving without my permission. My wrist flicked in circular motions, trying. The sides of my fingers pressed into the paper, the charcoal in hand.

I drew a dark black circle on white paper, but beneath all that darkness, I could see the outline of a face that once was. A face that looked like my own, but with buttons for eyes. Underneath that were words. Latin words. *Memento mori. Memento mori. Memento mori.*

And then a long croaking sound, and a movement buried in the pit of the corner.

I gasped, but I wanted to scream and yell, my fingers trembling.

I pushed away from the desk, the chair catching on the carpet and tipping me over. A whimper scurried from my body, and the sound was loud enough to stop the croaking in the corner. The croaking that was getting louder with vibrato but was now gone.

Couldn't look behind me. Didn't want to know what was inhabiting this room.

I tried to catch my breath. Tried to slow my breathing, and when I did, I pried the compressed charcoal pencil out of my hand and held my arm to my chest.

What the fuck was happening to me?

I hurried to the bathroom, almost tripping out of the room and turning on all the lights as I moved. I pulled off my shirt. My arms were covered in black from the drawing, and I pumped the soap vigorously into my hands with tears stinging my eyes. Turned on the hot water and scrubbed until the blackness swirled down the drain.

TWENTY-TWO

Daddy used to say that monsters couldn't hurt me.

Funny he'd say that, because right after, he and Bubba would come into my room once I'd dozed off and try to scare me with that stupid werewolf mask Daddy had gotten for Halloween.

My cousins hated staying over because they were so terrified of it. He kept it tucked in his closet, and after a while Bubba started using it, trying to scare me just as Daddy had, but it was only a mask.

I'd always known who was underneath it.

It was always someone I loved.

But that mask was left behind, at our old house, probably tossed in a dump now.

TWENTY-THREE

PRESENT DAY: MARCH

It was the middle of the school week, and I was exhausted.

Too afraid to enjoy shutting my eyes at night because of the fear that I might wake up somewhere else . . . or doing something else.

There was something dark and wrong with me. The dark place was sucking out my humanity like a leech on the small of my back.

I didn't know how much of me was fully my own. And when I went there, to the dark place, was I bringing pieces of it back here with me? Pieces that I couldn't see, couldn't feel, couldn't touch, but that would wreck me all the same?

I tried to research alternate universes that were gruesome and consuming. Tried to research how to stop myself from getting stuck. Even Google couldn't help me with this one. I was at least hoping for a database with bad advice, but all I could find were paradoxes.

I did come across a quote from Kurt Vonnegut's *Slaughterhouse-Five*. While it wasn't true for my life, it also wasn't untrue. And it was the only absolute thing that made me stop.

All moments, past, present, and future, always have existed, always will exist. . . . It's just an illusion here on Earth that one moment follows another one, like beads on a string, and that once that moment is gone it is gone forever.

It was similar to what Grandmommy said, so it had to mean something.

Sarah and I hung out in the art studio after school. I didn't want to be home alone, and I wondered if she sensed that. She had to finish up an art project that was due on Monday, and since I didn't have any upcoming assignments to work on, I put on an apron, grabbed some recycled clay, and headed to a pottery wheel.

Sarah hummed while she drew at the table, her earrings dangling. Quite frankly, the humming wasn't all that great—it was actually very much off-key—but she smiled while she hummed, and I wished I were like that. I wished I were honest with myself, free the way Sarah allowed herself to be.

"Can I ask you for advice?" I said, and she raised her brows, mischief in her eyes.

"Do you need me to show you how to feel up a boob again?"

I looked around, afraid Mrs. Jesse was going to come around the corner and scold us. "Oh my God."

She laughed and shrugged. "Eh, pish posh."

I rolled my eyes.

Sarah cleared her throat. "Advice, you say? What kind?"

"I'm curious—how are you so fearless all the time?"

"Darling..." she started, elongating the word, and she set her pencil down. "I'm happy you asked, but also, what makes you think I'm fearless?"

I didn't want to say it was the way she dressed sometimes. How she mixed patterns with bright colors and wore earrings with explicit words on them because that was how she was feeling that day, or because of the stories she told me of kissing whoever she wanted at camp one year just because she could.

I faltered, not saying anything, because I was afraid that if I did, I'd lie. I didn't want to lie to Sarah, not unless I had to.

She answered anyway. "You know, I don't know. Part of it is me not caring enough about what the world around me thinks. Which, I know, *big* surprise. But also, a lot of the time, I *am* scared.

Sometimes scared shitless, to be frank. But I do the thing anyway because it's the quickest way to conquer it."

"Thanks for that."

"Anytime, doll. Anytime."

TWENTY-FOUR

PRESENT DAY: MARCH

The doorbell rang just as I was about to mindlessly scroll social media in an effort to forget all the chaos that was happening to me.

I froze, realizing that all my family stayed down in Kansas City and Grandmommy always came in through the garage when she got off work, so I was unsure who could be here.

Got up and took two steps forward. Glanced around the corner to see if I could make out who the figure was outside by squinting and hoping that the frosted windows on the sides of the door

All I saw was a slender shadow moving side to side, with dark colors on and maybe dark brown skin?

Wait, was that . . . Eilam?

Duh. He knew where I lived, but we hadn't really talked about hanging out, unless—well unless he was coming over to tell me his secret.

The doorbell rang again, and I watched the figure readjust. I checked my phone for a text, but no, nothing.

I sighed and just went to answer it. It would suck if it was someone trying to sell me something—unless it was Girl Scout cookies. Ugh, yeah. I could really go for a cookie right about now.

Eilam was on the other side. A slanted smile in the corner of his lips, and he raised a hand. "Hey . . . uh, sorry I didn't text. Was trying to be spontaneous, but now I feel like this—me being here—is weird."

I almost laughed but didn't. "Yeah, it's a little weird."

In Eilam's other hand, and smooshed into his chest, were some sort of books. He looked past my shoulder, into the house, and I stepped out and shut the door behind me. There was no need for him to get any ideas.

"What's that?" I eyed the books in his hands. "Are you on your way to the library?"

"No, and—" He paused. Took a step back to take in the sight of me. "You really aren't one for small talk, are you?"

I shrugged. "Life is . . . unfortunately too short to focus on the mundane."

"What if what's mundane to you *isn't* mundane to someone else?"

"Are we speaking on the subject of art or what's tucked in your arm?"

He twisted his body away from me when I stretched my neck to see what he was hiding. "We're speaking broadly."

I hummed, the sound vibrating my lips, and I walked past him, sitting on the porch step. Eilam followed, still hiding away what he had, and it slightly annoyed me. Was it so bad to want to know right now?

"Okay, well, art is subjective, but so is mundanity."

He looked at the neighborhood, that smile still there, and I tried to follow his gaze, but I didn't think he was staring at anything. I think he was contemplating what he'd say next.

But I couldn't take my eyes off him, and I also couldn't wait for him to speak. He was processing at a rate too slow to keep my mind from wondering what would happen next. "Are you here to tell me your secret?"

"You didn't forget about that?"

"Did you forget about me disappearing?"

He looked at the stoop we sat on. Was he blushing? There was a subtle flush in his face, and as he continued to withhold eye contact, something about him made me feel like I knew him. It was as if this moment had happened before. As if I'd seen him in my dreams or some stored memory bank.

"I swear, it feels like I know you."

"How so?" He looked up, his gaze so focused on me it made me want to recoil, but I didn't.

"It's. I don't know. It's . . . I think it was just something about this moment that made me feel like I'd been here before—like I'd sat on the porch beside you." And more: Like I'd stared into his eyes longer than this now. Like he'd reached his fingers to my face to brush my bangs away before he placed a hand on my neck. Before he kissed my collarbone.

The thought of it made me warm. My toes tingled, and I wiggled them, pressed them into the concrete, hoping the feeling would go away.

"Why aren't you afraid of me?"

"Should I be?"

Yes, yes, he should be—but I didn't tell him that. Instead, I said, "It seems like a normal response. It's not every day you meet someone who time travels."

He grinned, looked away again, and he was about to say something. His lips parted, his tongue clicked, but then his phone chimed. When he checked it, his arms relaxed. For the first time I could see what he'd been hiding. Comic books.

"I actually have to head out. I'm on Julius duty tonight. My mom, she works the night shift."

I sat up a little. Julius. I remembered his laugh and his spiraling curls. "What does your mom do?"

"She's a doctor. She delivers babies."

"Wow, that's kind of a big deal . . ." I mumbled, thinking of my own parents. I should text them. Reach out. But I didn't even know if they'd answer—after all, the last time I saw them, they were afraid of me.

I tried not to think about it, but then the warmth grew into a gnawing and the gnawing grew into a sharp stabbing pain, turning my fingertips red. This was always the first sign. I knew that so much better now. The tingling came right before I disappeared. I didn't want to time travel, but how would I stop it?

"Yeah, she likes it a lot. She says it's exhausting, but it's worth it." He stood up. "You okay?"

I gulped. *No*, I thought, and I pressed my palms into the concrete, swallowed the slime in my throat as my heartbeat accelerated. "Yeah," I lied, and I hated that I did that. I needed to stop doing that.

There was a delayed response. He was measuring me, but then he placed the comic books in my lap, and I swear—I swear on everything, the weight of the paper resting on top of my thighs grounded me. The tingles faded.

"Marvel Zombies?" I asked, looking at the cover.

"You've heard of Marvel, right?"

I laughed. He couldn't be serious. "Who hasn't?"

"Right, but did you know that before the movies and TV shows, there were comics? It's genius because the whole Marvel universe is never-ending and expanding as we speak."

"Okay..."

"*Okay?*" He said it like I was missing the whole point, his eyes all wide until he exclaimed, "At the end of '05, Marvel released a limited series set in an alternate universe where the superheroes were all infected by the 'hunger,' which turned them into zombies. My grandpa bought the series for me right after I was born—all five of them. They're right there. You have to be careful with these, but you can borrow them. I wanted you to know that alternate realities...they're not as strange as you think. You're not, um, alone."

He started to back away then, and all I could do was rub my thumb over the Hulk and swallow the plummeting feeling that Eilam wanted me to feel like I had something.

"Julius has been asking about you. He's still up to play Smash."

I smiled at him. "You sure it's not you wanting to play Smash?"

That look again—the one that made me feel like there was more to us. And if time travel was only memories, then I needed someone to tell me where he fit in the equation.

"Bye, Hylee. Take good care of those comics. I'll be coming back for them," he said, and then he was swallowed by the sun and his white car.

I watched him drive away with the monstrosity thick in my lap, and the thought that if he hadn't been here, I'd be gone by now.

TWENTY-FIVE

The tingling ran down the outside of my arms like I was standing against a cold iron vent. I tied a scarf on my head in preparation for bed, staring at my reflection in the bathroom mirror, willing myself to stay here. Until I vanished.

Everything vanished.

It was deafening silence and my own heavy breathing.

I tried to exhale, but my insides felt compressed. Like I'd been dropped at the bottom of the undiscovered sea. I was being squeezed, and morphed, and pulled until I was nothing.

And I wanted to be nothing. I wanted so badly to have some

control over this menacing reality, and I wanted to cry—my throat so tight I thought my lungs had collapsed.

I landed.

Felt my knees scraping against the rough surface, and the tears came. I fumbled to my butt, my vision not quite there as I found my back pressed against a wall, my head falling into my lap as my ears popped.

Inhale. Exhale.

Then a smell came. Garlic and onions sautéed on a stovetop. Melted cheese cooling on top of a casserole. Hot grease with the smell of Cajun seasoning and paprika.

My stomach woke, making a sound. It was Mama's cooking. I knew that with absolute certainty, and even with my eyes closed, the saliva in my mouth tripled. I had to be home. And home... it was only a construct now.

Mama loved to cook. She loved experimenting, writing down recipes, watching specials on TV. When Bubba was around, I used to love cooking with her. Tossing the chicken into the seasoned flour. Listening to the way it popped in the hot grease on the stove. Mixing up the cornmeal for cornbread.

We used to be a home, and this smelled like that, but I...

I was afraid.

Too afraid to open my eyes, too afraid to discover where I'd been brought to this time. And I knew it was home, but not really.

Not *really* home . . . not *really* Mama's cooking.

There was a *hush, hush*. Mumbled whispers at first. Voices projecting in front of me, but not directly to me. My eyelids quivering. *Just open them*, I told myself, but I froze.

What if this was all a trick?

A dim light wavered, someone moving nearby, and the voices slid into familiarity. They weren't talking to me, or even about me, they were talking to each other. And I knew those voices, but they were haunted here. They sounded brittle and breathy, like they'd been speaking for decades but never stopped for water.

Another twitch, and I forced my eyes open. I was in the dark place, at my childhood home. *My home. My home. My home.*

My everything, all of it, somehow revived again. Though there was light, it was muted. Gray hues painted almost every surface, and darkness spilled from every crack and corner. The shadows inched toward the trim and ceiling like long, bony fingers, stretching like threads of loose hair.

The wooden bed frame to my right grew velvety mold in the spirals. Not quite right. My old blankets on the floor. My small desk covered in springing moss and loose dirt, the carpet a mix of different-sized vines and twisted dandelions.

In the center of it all stood a woman who looked like my mother—if my mother's dark brown skin were withered and gray like an elephant, and if her black hair were strawlike and flicked off her shoulder in stiff movements with each turn.

Like the girl I'd seen before, Mama's eyes were erased with smooth skin. No eyelashes, no eyebrows. Full lips twisted with thorns and bruises and pain, stretching across her grim face.

When she spoke, it was long and serious. Something she'd said before—one too many times—and I could tell that she was tired of saying it. Rage fueling her.

"Hylee," she said, and my eyes widened as I leaned forward, my mouth propped open.

And a smaller voice. Still as tired. Still as angry. *"Mama,"* she pleaded, and that little girl was me.

She was *me*. But how?

She was me, sitting on the ground, sheets spread out around her, and I missed it the whole time. Maybe I'd been too afraid to stare at her for long enough to notice, but that face. That voice. That was mine. So maybe she was the past version of me in this twisted universe?

It had to be that.

"You gotta pick up the pace." Mama spoke again, and it hurt to hear her talk. I wanted to cover my ears, but this felt like . . . it felt like they were here for me? Or were they? But I'd been here before—this moment wasn't new.

"You were supposed to do this thirty minutes ago," Mama said, and she took a step forward, head moving in my direction.

I pressed myself into the corner, my heart racing, thudding in my ears until I realized she didn't notice me—neither of them did. She kept speaking to the younger version of myself, and I was a ghost in their dimension, sitting on the floor, against the wall with the window blowing in cool air that smelled of wet earth.

Little Hylee huffed, her twisties moving as she picked up a comforter from the pile on the floor. "Mama, I'm hurrying, but the blankets have to go on in order."

Mama crossed her arms in front of her ribs and tapped her foot hurriedly. "When I come back, this better be done."

When Mama left, she closed the soot-covered door, and I watched little Hylee make her bed with my knees pressed to my chest, wondering if I moved, would I ruin anything?

As I watched her, I had this urgent, ticking feeling inside me that made me want to jump to my feet. That made me wonder again why this felt so familiar.

But then a pillow fell, and as Hylee went to pick it up, the sound of someone banging on wood made us freeze. It wasn't the bedroom door; it was one farther away.

Out there . . . past the hallway . . . The front door.

She looked at the bedroom door, and I followed her gaze.

Another bang. Louder, the sound echoing in the room.

A shout from the living room. A shuffle. Silence, and then: "*Who is it?*" I recognized the deep voice. It was low, a tremble crawling around it, uncertainty everywhere.

Little Hylee stayed paused like she was listening, her chest rising and falling quicker than it had been moments ago.

And it clicked.

Today was November 9. Today was the day Bubba disappeared. Which also meant that somewhere, *somewhere*, he was here, too.

There was a loud splitting sound, and I remembered it was someone kicking in the front door. It made both of us—me and little Hylee—flinch at the same time. I hopped to my feet, my toes pressing into the vine-covered carpet, the clematis crawling toward the corners.

Little Hylee inched closer to her bedroom door, slow, quiet steps, and I mimicked her, becoming her shadow. My shoulders low. My breath uneven. We heard another voice then. It was muffled but still loud. A man shouting. I didn't know who he was, but the way he sounded . . . the way his voice cracked through the opening of these ruined walls . . . it made me believe he was here for something awful. A price to be paid. Blood to be spilled.

Shots were fired and glass shattered. I rushed to the doorknob before the other version of me could, and as soon as I touched it to turn it, she did, too.

Her hand was cold, right beneath mine. We heard our name out there. Someone was searching for us. That voice. I remembered that voice.

The ice-cold air in my face as we swung the door open, my curls rustling. I was ready to run, but as I moved forward, everything turned black.

The nausea rushed in as I disintegrated, the world picking me up and spitting me out.

I landed on the floor, in my bedroom at Grandmommy's house.

My knees bounced on the carpet as I rolled into full existence again. I couldn't move. My eyes opened and watered as I saw flashes of the house playing out in my head.

Bubba had to be behind that door, in the house somewhere. I just knew it. He had to be. He *had* to be.

TWENTY-SIX

PRESENT DAY: MARCH

After the time traveling episode, I couldn't sleep. I kept the over-head light and the lamp on. I was sick of shadows.

I spread the comics out in the middle of my bed, and I read them one by one. I kept dozing off, but the sound of the banging and shots from the dark place woke me back up every time.

Soon, I learned about Earth-2149, and I read about Magneto, Black Panther, Wolverine, and Luke Cage. I learned how the Hunger made good people do awful things, and I learned that

My alarm sounded before the sun came up, and after I brushed my teeth and washed my face, I waited for the text from Sarah. She'd offered to be my ride to and from school like a freaking angel.

My head throbbed as I dragged myself to her Audi and hopped in.

"Shit, girl . . . you look like shit."

I smiled and buckled in. "At least I don't smell like shit."

She backed out of the driveway. "No, you smell like flowers that grow on holy land." I laughed, and she cleared her throat. "But all jokes aside, is everything okay?"

I wanted everything to be okay, and I really wanted to tell Sarah about all the chaos happening in my life. A part of me felt like she'd understand, but that other part—the nasty, raw, oozing part—felt like she'd run away terrified and confused. Just like Lucia.

So I swallowed the truth and shared a lie. "Yeah, everything's okay. Life is just"—and I stuck my tongue out—"life." And I hoped that'd suffice.

Sarah grinned. Sort of. "How about coffee, on me?"

"I literally love everything you're saying right now. Yes, a million times, yes!" I said, and Sarah turned up the music, put on her sunglasses. She belted out words to a song, and I smiled to try to keep from crying.

While she ordered for us, I pulled out my phone and sent a text to Eilam:

So about smash…

*

Eilam texted me back immediately. No surprise there. He said he'd pick me up from my school at exactly 3:15 p.m., and here's the kicker—he even offered to get me coffee.

Before I knew it, Eilam's old Pontiac chugged to the curb outside Lee's Summit West. He rolled down his window before he unlocked the door, and I bent down to see his smiling face.

"Are you ready for infinity and beyond?"

"I didn't realize Buzz Lightyear was picking me up."

That smile again. *And Jesus.* "Make no mistake, you're Buzz in this situation. I'm Sox."

He unlocked the door, and I dropped my backpack on the floor and slid in. "Why is that?"

"Because you're definitely the main character in this story."

I rolled my eyes. God. The boy was so cheesy.

We listened to Frank Ocean as we drove toward town center, entering downtown Lee's Summit. Today, the air was warmer. It reminded me that spring break was next week, and I'd told Mama and Daddy I'd come home this weekend.

After I texted Mama the other day, she called. Her voice sounded tired, but she seemed excited. I was on speakerphone with her and Daddy, and even when they told me about all the things I'd missed out on, I could still hear the concern under the words they didn't say. Another thing I noticed—they never asked me how I was. I didn't think it was to be malicious; rather, they seemed anxious about what I'd say when I answered the question.

We were on a sidewalk where the buildings hugged each other and shared large glass windows. We passed a barber shop, some boutiques, a Mexican restaurant on the corner, and then we stopped at a bakery and coffee shop, the Bibliobean.

I paused at the door as he opened it. "You mean to tell me you go to coffee shops that *aren't* where you work? That's wild."

Eilam narrowed his eyes as the small bell above the door chimed. "You'd be surprised at all the things you don't know about me."

"Oh, like your big secret?" I teased, and he moved forward.

I had another smart remark, but I was distracted by the sweet smell of cinnamon and vanilla that engulfed the air and rested on my tongue.

My stomach growled at the sight of everything. Brown, flaky

rolls drizzled with icing. Huge chocolate chip cookies and pistachio bars. Chocolate-filled croissants and slices of crumbly coffee cake.

Eilam leaned in to whisper, his voice pricking the hairs on my neck. We looked at each other, our noses inches away while I waited for him to talk, but all I could focus on was his lips.

Then a voice on the stage, past the small tables and chairs, stole my attention. They projected with confidence. A poetry reading.

He leaned away. "It's Pi Day. They always have an event and special pies available."

We walked to the glass case, the light inside making all the breaded things sparkle. We played off each other—quietly oohing and ahhing as we peered into the case. "What are you gonna get?" he murmured.

"It's on you, right?"

"Uhhh, yeah?"

"Okay, I'll take one of everything."

He laughed, and a lady from behind the counter approached, a finger over her mouth. We apologized, and she asked if we were ready to order. I decided on the cinnamon roll, solely because it was the biggest thing in there, draped in icing, and Eilam chose the chocolate croissant.

I told him I'd pay for both of them. He was surprised, but I was on a mission: I wanted Eilam to tell me his secret, and

I wanted to know if he knew anything about controlling time travel. I didn't have Iron Man or Dr. Strange around to build me a time machine.

We sat at a small booth with a dimmed light above us. The audience applauded the person who was onstage, and then someone announced how they were going into an interlude. Music began to play, and it reminded me of something Sarah had played in the car the other day. We didn't talk at first, we just exchanged flustered looks and smiles. But then, because of course I couldn't help myself, I cut right to the chase.

"What else do you know about time travel?"

"I know that it's confusing," he said.

"How so?"

"Wait...wouldn't you agree that it's confusing?" He wiped his mouth with a napkin.

"Yeah. It's fucking awful."

He grinned.

"But from what you've read or whatever," I said, steering the conversation back, "why do *you* think it's confusing?"

"It's confusing because there are multiple theories on the subject, with many of those theories coming from people who don't have the ability to time travel. Did I tell you that my grandpa is the reason I know so much about time travel?"

That was a weird pivot, but I said, "No..."

"He was, and he was a science professor at the University of Kansas, but he loved studying black holes and quantum physics, and it's why I know so much about it. While some theorists believe time is an illusion, my grandpa once said: *We are always going. Time doesn't stand still for anything or anyone. You cannot plead with it. It is not forgiving. It is not angry. It* is. *And even after we're gone, it will continue to be,*" he said. "And so, I also believe time travel is confusing because if time, as a construct, will always *be*—then how will we know all the answers?"

My jaw almost dropped. Multiple truths—that's what Grandmommy had said. Then I wiped my mouth before I said, "Wow," because Eilam's grandpa knew so much. He was a science professor who studied time travel, and what better person to speak to about this? "I'd love to meet your grandpa," I said, and as soon as I did, I realized how weird that sounded. "Not that you don't know things—it just sounds like he knows *more*." Fuck. That sounded weird, too. "But also, I'm sure you know a lot, too."

"No, no. He does—well, did—know more than me. So much more. My grandpa was a genius. But, um, unfortunately, he passed away a couple years ago."

"Oh. Shit. I'm sorry, Eilam."

"No, don't worry about it. My grandfather was a man who left a mark. It feels like he's still kicking around, even when he shouldn't be."

I smiled, and Eilam wiped his mouth with a paper towel. "You all done?"

I nodded.

"Great, time to pick up Julius!"

We were out of there, sugar on our lips, to-go coffees in hand.

TWENTY-SEVEN

Just like before, we pulled into the driveway of a fancy house.

Eilam explained that his brother had a different dad, Duke, and Duke was a dermatologist at a private practice. It just so happened that his mom and Duke met through the medical grapevine.

Also like before, Eilam climbed out the car, asked me to wait, and returned with a bouncing Julius on his hip. Except Julius looked as happy as ever. His finger pointed to me, and I waved at him through the window, and he squirmed around, holding tightly to his brother and a Grogu plush toy.

"Um, Lee!" Julius said as Eilam buckled him in.

"Um, Julius!" I said back.

He breathed fiercely, and he kept moving around, even after Eilam was all "Bubs, *please*. Just let me get you buckled in."

It came out with a squeal at first. "Are you gonna come to my house and we are gonna play Smash?"

I nodded, and Julius's mouth dropped.

"Are you excited, Bubs?" Eilam asked.

We were backing away from the house now, and Julius didn't know what to say, he just stayed there, his mouth open and his hands squeezing Grogu's ear until he busted into laughter. We laughed with him, and it was such a surreal feeling. I'd forgotten that little humans could be capable of so many emotions.

Eilam's house was in a cute neighborhood lined with different-sized homes. An elderly couple sat on a porch swing, hands interlocked. A few houses down, a woman with a sunhat mulched an empty garden bed on the side of her house. Next door to Eilam's home, a few kids played pickup ball, sweat glistening on their foreheads, bottles of water lying in the grass.

We parked in front of a ranch-style house with gray siding and black panels and a huge window that overlooked what I imagined was the living room.

I held our coffees while Eilam tamed and released the monster that was Julius, and I wondered if Eilam saw me holding my breath as we walked down the path to his front door. Could he tell that I was a bundle of anxiety?

Eilam's home smelled of clean laundry and new carpet. As soon as Eilam set him down, Julius took off running, falling briefly before getting up again.

Eilam flipped on a lamp, and we saw a note pinned to the corkboard by the entryway that said, I'LL BE HOME AT 6! ☺

The house opened up to a living room, the dining room behind it and the kitchen to the left of that. I looked around, taking in an island, a fridge, cabinets, and . . . Julius trying to grab something from the counter.

"Aht!" Eilam shouted, and took off after his brother.

To the left, past the kitchen, there was a hall lined with doors, one cracked open a hair. I imagined the bedrooms and bathroom were that way.

Julius went running, and Eilam chased after him, yelling to me that he'd be right back and that I could hang my jacket by the door.

All I could focus on was how immensely jealous I was of Eilam and his family. Could I stay here forever?

After some time, they came back—Eilam taking off Julius's jacket, and Julius tumbling onto the floor in the living room, kicking off his shoes, and pulling off his socks.

"Do you like having a brother?" I asked, and he nodded.

"I don't know if you've noticed, but it's a blast!"

Julius took off to grab a small green bucket in the corner of the living room.

Eilam shook his head and mouthed, "He's a monster!" before smiling again.

Julius brought me the bucket, his toes curling into the carpet. "Smash! We get to play Smash!"

Eilam and I joined him on the floor.

Julius's grin was full of drool, and some of it spilled out of his mouth as he dumped the bucket and all its contents onto the rug.

Small trucks and cars came tumbling out. I oohed and ahhed while he giggled.

"So here are the rules to the game," Eilam began. "You get to choose two cars. If the opponent smashes your car before you move it, you lose the car, and it goes back in the bucket. We do this until every car is back in the tub."

"What you're saying is that this is a glorified version of cleaning?"

Eilam smiled, and I wanted to fold over onto this floor. "My mom invented this game. Can you tell?"

Julius started smashing cars before we were ready, so we grabbed our two cars quickly and tried to move them before Julius smashed them.

We did this for a while. Julius laughing up a storm and having a blast, and I found myself having fun, simply because he was.

When I heard a garage door opening, I looked to Eilam, who said, "It's my mom. She knows you're here." I took a thankful breath and stood up to meet the woman who had birthed Eilam.

Eilam stood, too, and I was nervous. I'd kissed a number of boys, but I'd met none of those boys' parents.

I had *not* kissed Eilam, though the more time I spent with him, the more I thought about what it might feel like to press my lips against his lips. What would they taste like? Would I melt into him, and would he like it?

But anyway, I hadn't kissed him. He was a new friend, and now I was meeting his mother, so what did any of this mean?

Keys jingled, and Eilam elbowed me. "Are you nervous?" he whispered to me.

I couldn't even look at him while I responded. I just said, "Yes," while I stared, still waiting.

Eilam said, "She's gonna ask if you want to stay for dinner. You should say yes...but also, you have every right to say no...but *also* also, she's making pasta tonight, and it's the best thing in the world. Yup. I'm biased, but it's true."

I elbowed him back because I wanted him to stop talking, and then a tall woman with dark brown skin emerged from a door at the corner of the dining room. She had long black hair, wore blue scrubs, and juggled a purse, a lunch bag, and a binder.

"Oh, hi!" She almost sang the words, smiling with super white teeth and placing items on the dining room table.

Julius ran to her, and she scooped him into her arms, kissing him all over his face and hugging him, telling him how much she missed him, asking how he was.

I wondered what that feeling was like.

My parents didn't believe in physical affection in the way I'd come to realize I needed it. There were comforting words when I was sad, and hugs when Bubba never returned. There were shoulder pats while I stared out the window for hours as a child, thinking if I stayed long enough, I'd see my brother jump out of a police car with a smile on his face. Once he got inside, he'd say, *I was lost, and they finally found me!*

Of course, that never happened, and I spent many days in our first apartment after that house looking out the window in vain.

They'd pat my shoulder twice. *I'm here,* I think is what they wanted to say. *I'm here. I'm here.*

I waved, and Julius pointed to me. "You must be Hylee," she said, walking over now.

"Lee!" Julius shouted, bouncing on her hip.

"Lee? Her name is Hylee," she muttered to Julius.

"Lee," he said again.

"It's okay. I don't mind being called Lee." It was something I missed, actually. Didn't hurt as much hearing it now that Julius had said it a few times. Even if it tore small slits in my heart, it would only ever hurt if salt got in the wound.

"Lee it is then. It's so nice to meet you. Eilam has said great things." She gave me a side hug, and Julius touched one of my curls.

"Really?" I said, and after we parted I caught the end of Eilam miming "cut it out" to his mom.

She laughed, and she squeezed Eilam into a hug and planted a kiss on his cheek. Then she pinched his chin. Julius tried to do the same. "He's getting old on me," she said, smiling, and Eilam's eyes were big, only staring at his mom. A look that said she was embarrassing him, but I thought it was cute.

"Your home is beautiful," I said, and I meant it. She had so many photos of the boys on her walls. Eilam hadn't changed much since he was a kid; he just looked like he'd stretched out into the person he was today.

"Thank you. I quite like it myself. You can call me Audrey, by the way. I'm not old enough to be called anything else. But how about dinner? I'm planning on making chicken fettuccine and garlic bread."

All three of them stared at me with the same eyes. Big, round, warm, and inviting. I couldn't say no to them, but also, I really didn't want to.

"I'd love to stay for dinner," I said, meeting their eyes with a smile, and as soon as I committed, I took out my phone and texted Grandmommy.

After dinner, Audrey asked if I wanted to stay for their family movie night. Again, I couldn't say no. She said they tried to watch a movie together once a week. Since Julius wouldn't stop talking about it, she figured why not and that I could cast a vote in what we watched.

However, Julius had a pretty solid argument about why he wanted to watch *Finding Nemo*, and while the majority of his delivery consisted of gibberish and slobber, I was totally taken by his reasoning (his reasoning being literally, "I want to see Nemo"), and before I knew it, I was sitting on the couch, the lights off save for a small lamp, Julius tucked in right between Eilam and me.

He smelled like Cheetos Puffs and pasta, and I was partially nervous that he'd get his sticky fingers all over my jeans, but then Audrey called him over to her rocker. "Bubs, come on over here." She kissed him on his forehead and folded him into her lap. Was Mama like that with Bubba when he was little?

Eilam scooted closer to me. My right arm pressed against his left one. It was a warm contrast. He grabbed the fleece blanket from the back of the couch and draped it over us.

I sank in, watching the bright colors on the screen and learning about anemones. I'd watched *Finding Nemo* before, but today, watching Nemo's dad hold him in his fins after their family home had been destroyed made my throat tighten.

Eilam pressed his thigh into mine beneath the blanket, and I looked at him. He kept his gaze on the TV, but his eyes sparkled, a small smile on his face.

Then his phone was out, and in the bright white box of his messaging screen, he typed: *Wanna text?*

Nodded, pulled my phone out, dimmed the light on the screen.

Hi

Hey

Are you having fun so far?

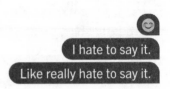

I hate to say it.

Like really hate to say it.

But yes. I'm very much enjoying myself.

You're always welcome here

Just so you know

It's like you knew I needed to see that

Are you psychic?

Lol I forgot to mention. I come from a long line of psychics.

Wait

Are you serious???

I'm literally joking

He laughed and I shoved him.

On a serious note. Everything ok?

This was where I needed to decide if I was going to be honest with Eilam. He already knew my secret, and yet, he didn't scold me or hide. I wanted him to be afraid because his fear would only confirm that what was happening to me was an inexplicable phenomenon. But he made me feel like my inexplicableness was worth being seen.

With a stranger, I felt worthy. With my family, I felt like I was worthless.

And yes, I understood that this was a dangerous place to be. Opening up makes it easy to get hurt. But if he was willing to be human with me, I wanted to do the same.

> Another honesty moment here
>
> But it's been rough
>
> Rough being an understatement
>
> I can fill you in later

Eilam started typing, the thought bubbles appearing on my phone, and then Audrey cleared her throat, giving us both a glare. Eilam slid his phone into his pocket beneath the blanket. I did the same. Then he weaved his warm fingers with mine, squeezing my hand. I squeezed his hand back, the pulse beneath his skin beating.

We stayed that way until the movie was over, and Eilam invited me to his room.

The first thing I noticed was all the comics. He had a bookshelf in his room filled with them. Posters covered the wall, and he had one of those cool static electricity balls plugged in. I rushed over to touch it, the purple light following my finger wherever it went.

Eilam sat on his twin-sized bed—the covers tucked in, folded nicely—his shoulders hunched over, his jaw loose as his hands rested in his lap.

"Do you want to be a comic artist?" I asked, looking at his comics and touching them. He didn't tell me to stop or feed me a fun fact about the comic my finger rested on. The silence felt incredibly loud, and I thought maybe he'd been distracted for a moment—it seemed as if Eilam always had something to say—but when I looked over my shoulder, I saw clearly that he was watching me with an intensity that made me squirm.

Then he said, "No, I don't want to be a comic artist, but I can see how you came to that conclusion. I've been thinking about being an audio engineer."

I swiveled, my back to the bookshelf. "An audio engineer, huh?"

He tugged on his curls, and suddenly I realized I wanted to do that. I wanted my fingers in his hair. "Yeah," he said. "I love music, but I love *the how* more. How the sound came to be how it is, and the idea of thinking I could have a hand in helping produce something great."

I was unsure how to respond besides the usual "That's great," because part of me felt guilty. I wished I'd known that about him sooner, and if it weren't for time traveling, I imagined I would have asked him that night of Kesha's party.

But also, if it weren't for the time traveling, would we be here today?

Eilam picked up his phone, pressed a few buttons, and then music filled the room. An older song with a slower tempo and a strong electric guitar. A silence between us again, like the first time we met. That familiarity of thinking I knew him, imprinted on me like a tattoo.

When I moved closer to him, I could sense it in my veins. Multiple histories merging together to create this moment.

His eyes followed me when I sat down beside him. Then he looked away. A shy grin slid into his lips.

"You don't have any fun facts for me today?"

"There's *always* something."

"And are you going to share it?"

He let his shoulders fall. "Maybe later."

"Why not now?"

"I'm beginning to think you're afraid of the silence between us." His eyes were low when he said it, focusing on my mouth.

I wanted to force him to look at me, to put my hand on his chin, make him stare me in the eyes until the uncomfortable felt comfortable.

After all, it felt like I'd done that before. Like we'd already been this close. "I'm not a big fan of silence," I finally said, and I stood up, got in front of him, my knees touching his knees.

Eilam looked at me with doe eyes, and I thought I might shatter. In a way, I did.

I fell into him, both my hands trailing over the sides of his face. My fingers in his soft curls.

Eilam pressed his arms around me, and I could feel his hands wrapping around my waist.

I lowered my head to his, my curls falling, creating a curtain. Our noses were close at first, warm air shared on both faces. And I looked him in the eyes completely, and he looked in mine the same. It was horrifying, seeing him this way.

And God, it was also absolutely and incredibly spectacular.

We kissed, and I liked the way my body was with his body.

How he slowly raised me up. How I let gravity take us, smashing us into the bed.

I liked the small giggle we shared between the uneven air in our lungs. The idea that this was a secret. I liked how this felt unending. We felt unending. And I wanted to dissolve into him.

In the smallest breath he broke away to say: "So then, ask me what my secret is."

His face hovered above me, our stomachs touching. I rested my head on his bed, reached out a finger to touch his chin.

My lips were sticky when they parted. "What's your secret?" I said, my words barely a whisper.

His brown eyes deepened, and he pressed his thumb to my collarbone, yet another thing between us that was achingly, impossibly familiar.

It was the catch of his breath that I heard before I heard the words themselves. Then, as clear as day, *"I'm a time traveler, too,"* he uttered.

And I gasped. Breathed in so quickly my chest hurt. That. That couldn't be true.

But then he disappeared—all his pieces swirled like an asterism around me, my curls catching in my eyelashes.

It was the best, and absolute worst, magic trick I'd ever seen.

TWENTY-EIGHT

I jumped out of the bed.

Eilam was not there. He'd disappeared like glitter dust in a tornado.

Was that what it looked like when I disappeared?

Another moment passed before he returned, and he appeared, standing at the edge of his room, a rouge tint in his face.

He smiled at me, took a step forward, and I retreated, stumbling.

He held out a hand. "Hey, you okay?" he asked. Eilam was a time traveler. That was his secret. This whole time, he could do what I could, and he didn't tell me. He didn't even realize what it would have meant to me if he had. Was that why he knew so much? Was that why he wasn't afraid?

"No, I'm not okay. You *lied*."

Eilam rushed over to me, placing his hands on my arms, and my teeth clenched. The water boiling inside me. "Don't touch me." The words rushed out in a wave; I was a pipe breaking. My vision blurring. It was too much. "You lied." And I flinched when I said it. *I was a hypocrite.* I knew that much, but it still stung. I'd decided to trust him, to be honest. And look where it got me.

He backed up. His facial expression changed from soft to something else. Fear, maybe? "I swear, it wasn't like that. I'm sorry I didn't tell you sooner. I wasn't sure how."

"The *moment* you knew about me . . . why didn't you think it was time then? Why wait? You knew my deepest secret. I trusted you with it, but you couldn't even trust me to tell me about yours. Why? You even acted as if you'd never met a time traveler before. Asking me all those questions, talking like it was only a theory to you before . . . but all this time, you could have told me. You chose to pretend. You're not sorry, Eilam."

His hands were limp now, his mouth agape, and he came closer. "I should have told you—*I should have*—the moment I found out. But I freaked, Hylee. I freaked out. *Shit*," he bellowed, dropping his hands. They had been in the air, lingering in space. "I was still trying to wrap my head around meeting you. Besides my grandpa, I didn't think there was anyone else. And when I wanted to tell you . . ." His shoulders leaned in. "It was already too late."

My cheeks were on fire now. "Your *grandpa*?!" I lowered my voice, remembering this wasn't my house, and I didn't want to disrespect his mother or wake his little brother. I pushed past Eilam and left the room.

I didn't see Audrey in the front room or kitchen when I left, so I grabbed my jacket off the hook by the front door, and I stood outside, trying to figure out which app I needed to download for someone to drive me home.

It only took a few minutes before Eilam met me outside, and even then, I didn't want to speak or look at him. "What are you doing?" he said.

"Why do you even care?" My voice was brash.

Since Eilam was taller than me, he saw what was on my phone. "Come on. Let me take you home."

I stared at him, my eyes big, and then he walked to his car and unlocked it. I was hesitant, but it was a free ride.

The moment I touched the door handle, Eilam said, "Seriously? That's it? You don't want to talk this out with me?" His voice was pleading, his eyes glossed even in the dark.

I didn't respond. I got in, and after a moment, he got in, too. It wasn't a fight I wanted to have with Eilam, but he didn't get that he'd hurt me. I knew more than anyone else that lies had always been daggers. And so many of them had already been thrown. My parents. Grandmommy. Lucia, and now Eilam. Just a list of people carrying wounds with my name in them. But somehow, that still hadn't prepared me for how much it hurt when someone threw their own lies at me.

My chest felt so heavy as he turned from road to road to road. I wanted to throw up, and I almost did at one point, lurching forward, Eilam's eyes on me, my fingers resting on the handle.

And he kept looking over at me the rest of the ride home, hoping I'd give him the chance to speak. Really, if he had something to say, he could have said it; I wasn't holding his tongue. I couldn't control him.

A small part of me, deep behind my navel, hoped. Hoped he'd talk to me, even if I was mad. Hoped he'd find me worth the effort, hoped he'd try. But then he pulled into the driveway and turned off the ignition.

I was out of the car within seconds, my curls twisting in the moonlight, and so was he. In front of me now, his hands on my arms. *"Please."* The word stretched between us, wrapping me up. "Give me a chance to explain myself," he murmured, and I didn't move at first. My body felt so weak and languid. And I wanted answers. Wanted to crack this fucking world open like an egg and watch the yolk spill and seep.

It wasn't just Eilam I wanted answers from, though. Grandmommy knew something, she had to. And my parents, *they* had to. And while I wanted to ask Eilam all of the things, now wasn't the time.

"Later," I managed to say. I could give him that because I absolutely wanted to talk to him later. This wasn't over.

His shoulders dropped, taking a breath.

Okay was probably what he thought, and he gave me a nod, moved out of my way, and I was gone.

TWENTY-NINE

It was the sound of cards falling and then a skid against concrete that scared me and my cousins. We were in the backyard playing catch, and the ball almost hit me in the face when I stopped to see what was happening.

Over there, past the gazebo, and in the driveway, were my parents, my older cousin Juice, a couple of family friends, and this guy I'd never seen before.

They were sitting at a card table, and the guy I didn't know banged his fist. The red pushed through his brown skin, and his eyes bulged. Direct points. "Man, where's my wallet?" he shouted.

They stared at him, Daddy scowling, his head tilted like me and my cousins.

The man puffed his chest, his nostrils flared, brows low as he backed away from the card table, the chair falling on the ground as he stood. "Damn, did I stutter? It was in my pocket and now it's gone, so who has it?"

"Hey, man, you need to chill out. I don't like you accusing my family of stealing. Ain't nothing like that going on over here."

"Don't tell me to chill out. I'm calm as fuck right now, but I'm about to go off. I'll say it again. Who has my wallet?" He pointed his hand at Mama's cousin, the other hand on his back pocket.

Daddy's eyes were big now, and I started breathing fast. My cousins huddled around me. We'd never been so quiet before—especially Asia, she was always talking about something.

"Was that a threat?" Daddy said, and he got closer to the guy.

The guy straightened his stare, and I saw that thing in his throat bob up and down.

"Look, we don't know where your wallet is, but I'mma need you to head out. We don't even know you. You can't come to my house acting square."

The man balled his hands into fists and sniffed. He took a few steps forward, running into the card table, and at the same time

Juice stood up, placing a hand on his friend's chest, trying to back him up. "Latrell, bro, it ain't worth it. Chill the fuck out."

Latrell didn't move, though, and his eyes widened when he slammed his fist on the table repeatedly. "Give. Me. My. Money." The words sliced through his teeth.

Daddy straightened his posture, his hands where I couldn't see them, and all of us kids moved forward slowly. "Leave," my dad said.

"Give me my money!" the man shouted again, and we all flinched. Shared a gasp.

Daddy put a hand to the man's chest. "Get the fuck outta here, man," he said, white spit going everywhere.

The man lifted the table, flipping it, the rest of the cards flying around everyone, drinks spilling. A roar ripped from his throat, and Daddy shoved him. He shoved back. One of Daddy's friends stood, trying to get Daddy to back up, and Juice tried to do the same thing with Latrell. They wouldn't relent.

Then one of my aunties rushed out the house, down the back porch. Past them, straight to us kids. "Don't look at them!" she shouted. "Go! Let's go!" She tried to get us to turn around. Tried to force us out the backyard, to the street so we wouldn't see Daddy and this stranger throwing hands.

And where was Bubba?

It had been a minute since he'd slipped away. He said he'd be right back. That he was hungry, but maybe he got bored of us kids. Maybe he was on the computer.

The last thing I saw before we were rushed out the backyard was the man spitting blood onto the driveway. Juice helped him off the ground and pulled him away from the house, but he fought it the whole time, barking bad words.

"You better watch your back," he said, and I swore I heard the words vibrate in the sky. Then they were gone, pulling away with speed in his dark car.

It was his eyes. A ticking time bomb. A firecracker. The way his words mixed with venom stuck with me and rattled me for days after that.

That night, it was hard to sleep alone, hard to crawl into my twin-sized bed and close my eyes because past the walls, outside, in the driveway, I could still hear that man. Could still see the red rippling across the whites, his pupils dilated in rage.

But what was worse than the sounds and sights that haunted me was playing hide-and-go-seek with Bubba a week later and finding a black leather wallet tucked under his bed against the wall. I'd never seen bills so big when I opened it. More hundreds than I could count. And inside the wallet, in front of the money, was an expired Kansas driver's license for Latrell Wood, the man who lost his wallet. The man who warned Daddy to watch his back.

THIRTY

It was the first Saturday of spring break, and I'd promised my parents I would come to visit, so here we were.

Grandmommy didn't stop the engine when we pulled into the driveway of the rental.

The white paint was chipped on the sides of the house, the shutters were a faded blue, and the black bars against the windows only rusted a little toward the tips. They were meant to keep people from breaking in, but what if the enemy was inside the

The concrete steps crumbled toward the sides, the yard mostly dirt where grass should be. Grandmommy said they needed to put hay down, salvage what they could if they wanted grass this spring and summer, but my parents didn't care. They didn't own it, and they probably wouldn't be here for longer than a year.

I couldn't help but think of Eilam's house, how clean and neat and warm it was, but I pushed that thought away. Thinking about the way we'd fought—the way I'd acted—would bring nothing but guilt, and I didn't have the energy to deal with that right now.

I huffed when I grabbed my bag from the back and shut the car door. I hated this place. It reminded me too much of my old neighborhood. Not that I hated my old neighborhood, but I hated what happened to us there, hated how we *weren't* there. Hated how my skin tried to peel away from my muscle with each step I took until I was face-to-face with the front door.

And last time I was here, we were a wreck.

I still remembered the tears that slipped past Mama's cheeks when she said goodbye to me a month ago. And the way Daddy squeezed me so tight, I thought my ribs would crack if I breathed too deeply.

When I rang the doorbell, I heard Mama shout on the other side, "It's open."

Daddy's eyes were the first thing I saw. Wide, the hazel glistening. Daddy had always been told he looked like Terrence

Howard. It was because he was light skinned and had light eyes, and those eyes were passed down to him from Grandmommy, but the resemblance stopped there.

If Mama had a celebrity look-alike, it was Taraji P. Henson, which worked out great for my parents because every Halloween they'd either be the characters from *Empire* or *Hustle & Flow*. But today, her eyes were red. Those eyes that were mirrored in my own face.

I was a mixture of both of my parents. I had Mama's high cheekbones and smile. The two of us, we could be twins almost, but I had Daddy's nose. He reminded me of that often, putting his thumb between his fingers. *Got your nose*, he'd say. It wasn't as funny as it used to be when I was five. And Bubba had been the exact replica of Daddy, minus the eyes. He'd inherited Mama's dark brown ones.

There were no jokes today, and if I'm being honest, there hadn't been any jokes for a while.

Inside was the same as it was the day I left. The air a mix of Fabuloso and something moldy wafting from the vents. It was probably from the water that had flooded the basement right after we'd moved in. The owner came to clean it out, but only after our family photos and memorabilia had been damaged far beyond repair.

It was funny, in a very noncomical way, how Daddy watched

Avengers: Age of Ultron. It reminded me of the comics and Eilam, how he was sort of obsessed. It reminded me of *me.* Endless time-lines stretching across a multiverse. It reminded me of how Eilam lied.

Mama sat on the white embroidered couch. Something a friend from work had given her after the last couch had broken from the previous move. And Daddy sat on the floor between her legs as she finished braiding his hair.

"Hey, sweet girl," Mama said, her smile taking up most of her face as she continued to braid.

I sat on the couch beside her, picking at the floral design of the fabric, feeling the thread of each petal beneath my fingertips. It was bumpy, the material catching on the edge of my ragged thumbnails. I sketched out the flowers once, at the beginning of my notebook. It was something to do besides being bored as hell if I wasn't working on an art project.

"Hey," I said, my smile timid. I was unsure how they'd be around me today. Were they still scared?

Daddy held his arms open. "Don't forget about me." His voice light, like he was up to something. I kneeled down to give him a hug, and he chuckled, trying to pull me into a headlock, and Mama popped him on the arm for moving too much. Said he needed to be still if he wanted her to finish up quickly.

I gave Mama a kiss on the cheek, returning to my seat before nudging Daddy in the side. It was something we did. Mostly because Daddy was awkward, and he didn't know how to say *I miss you*. He just knew how to roughhouse and throw a pillow at you. It was like he'd never grown up.

With a breath, I leaned into the couch cushion and watched some building explode in the movie on TV. From the corner of my eyes, I peered at Mama, trying to catch what was different, what felt off.

Mama was skinnier than the last time I'd seen her, her wrists frail and small enough for me to wrap my fingers around comfortably. Her brown skin seemed pale somehow, and I wondered if me disappearing caused her and Daddy to spiral out of control.

Spiral. It wasn't something that happened often, and they liked to think they had it all together. They wanted the world to see it that way, but I'd never forget how gone Mama was when Bubba disappeared. Weeks would roll into the next, and she'd sit frozen, not moving, not eating. And Daddy didn't sleep. He couldn't rest at the thought that someone could break in again, finish the job they'd originally set out to do.

Mama and Daddy tried to drink away the memories of having a son. It was also why they always had people over. A full house would forever mask loneliness. But in our cells, we'd always feel that violent stab of loss. It would be deep down, past the tissue and muscle. A pain that burned and made you want to burst into flames.

"Lee—" Mama started, and then cleared her throat, her eyes not meeting mine. "Hylee, go turn that oven on for me. Set it to three seventy-five."

My bottom lip folded under my teeth. It was on her tongue, *Lee*. A force in her, pushing the word out, but she swallowed it anyway, and I hated how she tried to erase part of my existence. How they all tried to erase it. I was *still* Lee. Did anyone here really *see* me?

"Daddy's gonna be starting up the grill here soon, too." And I wanted to ask why, but she answered for me. "We're having people over tonight." She smiled after she said it, but it was a straight smile, not a real one.

I huffed loudly, but I didn't talk back because I didn't want to be scolded. But . . . why the fuck were they having people over? Didn't they care that their daughter—who very much needed them—was back in town for the first time in a month? That the last time they had a party, I literally disappeared?

"Hy*lee*," Mama called after me, stretching my name like she did sometimes. I'd already hopped up to do as she asked. "Uh-uh," she continued. "What's with the attitude?"

My nostrils flared, my eyes watering as I turned on the oven. "Nothing," I lied.

Nothing.

The incense was burning, R&B music blasting from the TV, and I was back on the couch, texting Sarah, when Daddy plopped onto the seat cushion next to me.

"What you so smiley for? You talking to a boy, Hylee?" he said, cleaning the scuffs off his white Air Force Ones with an old toothbrush.

Shit. Like it mattered. Last time Daddy tried to sit me down to talk about relationships, all he could get out was *Don't do it.*

Didn't know what that meant. Just knew that I absolutely wanted to do the opposite of whatever he said. "It's a friend." My teeth were clenched when I said it.

He narrowed his gaze on me, and I saw Bubba there, in his eyes. It was only for a second, but I knew that look anywhere. Maybe Daddy would tell me what happened that night, maybe I could get some answers from him, but the moment I wanted to open my mouth, Mama called me into the kitchen.

"Check on those greens for me," she said when I got in there. She was chopping potatoes on the counter opposite the stove, but the kitchen was so small, it felt like we were basically rubbing shoulders.

Grabbed the ladle and opened the lid to stir, the smell of peppers hitting me straight in the face. I wasn't sure if it was done or not, but it smelled good.

"Here," Mama said. She placed the knife on the cutting board and moved to the fridge. "Finish chopping these potatoes for me. I need to make sure this chicken is ready to go on the grill for your daddy."

I closed the lid, washed my hands, and did as she said. Mama seasoned the chicken, throwing some salt past her left shoulder for good luck.

We worked in silence, but in my head, I heard the call of my name and the rush of those brown hands coming toward me. It reminded me of the night of the incident.

Mama. She was here. And she was there that night. If I asked gently, maybe she'd tell me this time.

"Mama." I braced myself, sucking in a deep breath of air. "Can you tell me what happened the night Bubba disappeared? I just, I can't re—"

"Hylee, no. We're not talking about this right now," she said, her voice like glass—cold and hard—and I gulped down that lump of sadness and pushed it into my belly.

The tears slipped out anyway, blurring my vision as I chopped the potatoes thin and tossed them into the pan in front of me.

THIRTY-ONE

After putting the potatoes in the oven, I wandered into my room here. The walls empty, the bed covered with a thin blanket. They probably let their guests use this room when I was away. They treated this place like it was some motel.

Didn't trust it, so I grabbed a towel from the hall, draped it over the bed, and played a game on my phone until my eyes grew tired, and I fell asleep with the sun shining through the window on my back.

The music woke me, my shoulders cracking around me as a barricade in this squeaky bed, protecting me. Winced, and when

I did, something didn't feel right. It wasn't that I'd time traveled. I knew that feeling too well now. It was different.

Rushed out of bed, something wrong.

Very, very wrong.

Bumped into a shoulder in the hallway, the voices of people laughing and eating.

Tears leaked like silk out the corners of my eyes as I hurried to the bathroom sink, and I didn't know why.

Panic inside my bones, sucking the marrow dry, and I felt my skin shriveling at my fingertips like I'd been in the tub for too long. Like I'd been forgotten about.

Hot water shot from the faucet when I turned it on, scaring me at first, and I cupped my hands, letting them fill before splashing the water on my face.

When my fingers swept past my skin, I felt the swelling in my lips. They were glued shut somehow, muting my screams. My voice trapped, the sound trying to claw its way out of my esophagus, but my lips would not part.

My chest heaved when I looked in the mirror: My once-brown eyes were blacker than the roots of my curls. I blinked. Then they were covered with coins that read *Memento mori*.

Another blink, and my lips twisted and twisted and twisted, thorns poking from the inside, vines rushing out my ears, blood spilling down my face.

Then.

The yellowed light in this bathroom flickered and dimmed slowly. The buzzing sound of flies running into something over and over again grew as the darkness crept from the shadows around me, climbing up the splits in the wall until there was a figure standing behind me, reaching to grab me, to consume me like it had already consumed everything else.

The fingers stretched for my shoulder, covered in moss, and it was the last thing I saw before everything went black.

I woke up with a start, the smell of moldy wood filling my nostrils as I heaved, trying to will the air back into my body.

I touched my face, my lips soft, warm. It wasn't ... it wasn't real. It was only a dream, but I still wanted to cry. And who would I turn to here? My dad, who hid from his emotions, or my mom, cold and hard?

But there *was* someone who'd listen to me. I just hadn't forgiven him yet.

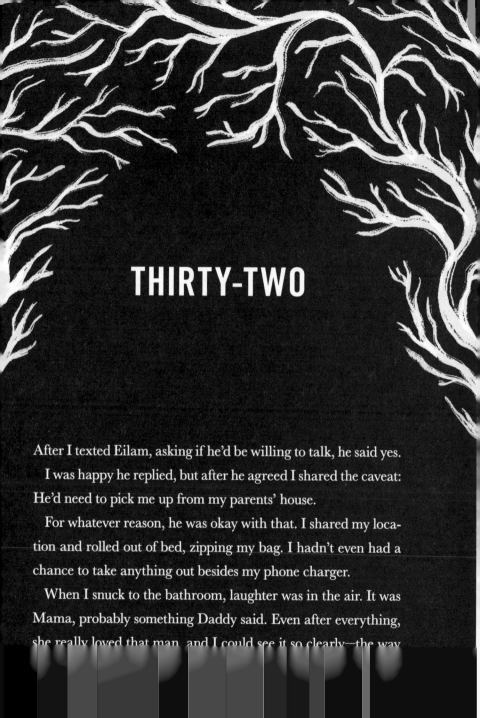

THIRTY-TWO

After I texted Eilam, asking if he'd be willing to talk, he said yes.

I was happy he replied, but after he agreed I shared the caveat: He'd need to pick me up from my parents' house.

For whatever reason, he was okay with that. I shared my location and rolled out of bed, zipping my bag. I hadn't even had a chance to take anything out besides my phone charger.

When I snuck to the bathroom, laughter was in the air. It was Mama, probably something Daddy said. Even after everything, she really loved that man, and I could see it so clearly—the way she looked at him when he told a joke to their friends, her dark eyes round and sparkling.

Had to wait to use the bathroom. Someone was in there. I crossed my legs as I leaned against the wall in the hall. A woman strolled out after, giving me a confused scowl like I shouldn't be here. Who was she to look at me like that? Even if I didn't want it to be, this was my house. Those were my parents, and no one should look at me like that. Not if they knew who I was.

Peed, washed my hands, and scrubbed my face. The image of how I looked in my dream still lurked behind my eyes as I patted my lips dry.

My heart raced, pulsing in the tips of my ears as I moved back to my room to put on my shoes and grab my things. It felt like I'd choke on my words if I spoke. Like I couldn't breathe. Like I couldn't do anything. But I needed to calm down. Eilam was on his way, and everything would be all right.

And there was a reason for all of this. I just needed to find it.

I went to where my parents were, at a table playing dominoes. The smell of liquor rose with each breath. Everyone yelled at one another over the music, and when Mama finally saw me, she smiled, motioning me over to give her a hug. At least when she drank, she was nice.

I whispered in her ear, "I'm leaving, headed back to Grandmommy's."

Her face didn't crumple as much as I thought it would. I'd only been here for a few hours. If I were her, I'd ask why. I'd tell me to stay. But she didn't ask those things. She patted her palm against my cheek gently, and then I moved to Daddy, giving him a hug as he yelled something to someone on the opposite end of the table.

Maybe they'd notice I'd left in the morning.

Outside, the sun had been long gone behind the houses in the distance, and a car rattled by, the music shaking their windows. It was eleven in the evening, but it felt so much later than that. A dog barked next door, and as I sat on the steps, I heard a Biggie song come on. Something like, *Now honeys play me close like butter play toast.*

Another car drove past, slowing down, and for a second, I thought it was Eilam. But it was some Ford Taurus, rolling down their window to shout, "Heyyy, mami," and I rolled my eyes as they sped away, grateful it was just that.

I flipped the car off once it was down the street, happy they didn't see me do it. I hated being catcalled, but some dudes didn't know how to handle rejection, and well, I'd hate to piss anyone off. Didn't want Daddy to have to get involved in anything while he was under the influence.

Finally, Eilam's Sunfire turned the corner, and I could see him stretching his neck to make sure he was at the right address.

Eilam.

I remembered the look on his face from the other day. How upset he seemed, and desperate to talk to me, to tell me how he felt.

I ignored that, pushed all those feelings down because he'd lied with everything in him, and if he knew the hell I'd gone through the last few weeks, maybe he'd feel the same.

But Eilam didn't know. I hadn't told him because I didn't think he'd understand, and now I felt my heart throbbing in my chest as I stood to walk to his car. Truth was, I felt bad about how I acted the other day. And now I was nervous to tell him this, but I needed to.

He got out, leaned against the driver's door. He didn't seem as eager as usual to see me. His eyes lit up for a moment and then dimmed, small wrinkles in the corners.

It looked like he'd slept but hadn't had rest. I'd been there before. I'd had nights where sleep wasn't sleep. Where every sound snapped your eyes wide open, and every breath had to be counted. The counting would bring the sunrise.

His hands hid in the front pocket of his black hoodie. Even from here, a small whiff of coffee drifted into my nostrils. And I could use that right now. I could wrap my limbs around him, nestle my nose deep into that scent. Let myself be free.

Instead, we stood still, facing each other and waiting.

I knew I should be the first to break the silence. I had to be, because I was the one who had cut him off before. But then he cleared his throat, the sound sharp in the evening.

"I'm sorry," he said, and I knew he meant it. There was no doubt because I felt his apology the night I found out he was a time traveler; I just couldn't stomach it then.

It was the fact that he'd been hiding it from me that hurt more than anything. Secret keeping was a theme in my life that I didn't want to be recurring.

"Hold on. Wait." The breeze picked up, and I had to force my curls back, the wind tickling my spine. "I know you already apologized, but I want to apologize, too, before we say anything else. I'm sorry for not giving you the chance to speak the other day. I was just so upset. Some of that was because of you, but most of it was the fact that my life is unfolding before me, and I can't get a grip on it. I'm either disappearing or someone's lying to me, and it's fucking exhausting."

He nodded.

"So I need you to know that I am upset with you, but it's not all because of you. I just don't get why you would keep that secret from me, Eilam. I mean, I get that it's scary . . . I do, but that reasoning seems so flat when you knew who I was the whole time."

He sighed. "No. You're right. It's a weak-ass excuse. I was afraid to tell you because I've done it before, and it's gone badly. I've told friends, and they thought I was losing it. I know you wouldn't have done the same, but... I don't know. I was still caught up in that idea, even if that wasn't true. You get me? My family knows, and I was going to tell you, I just wasn't sure how yet, and I was having so much fun with you. Besides my job at the coffee shop, you've been my excuse to get out of the house, explore. I haven't done that since my granddad passed away."

He looked past me, and I didn't think I'd ever assumed that Eilam was a homebody. To me, he seemed so worldly. "Being around you, Hylee, it changed my outlook on how I explored the world because... suddenly, I wanted to explore it with you."

I loosened my jaw, my mouth opening a little. For once, I felt speechless.

He started again, looking away now. "It... also doesn't help that you're kind of intimidating."

"Me? Intimidating?" I looked around the driveway, laughing at how little space I took up. "Wait. No. You're scared of *me*?"

A smile broke across his face, and I wanted to hold it there. I wanted to smile with him, look into his dark brown eyes and get lost. I didn't realize he'd felt the way he did, and maybe I shouldn't have been thinking these things, but it felt so good, and I just wanted to enjoy one moment. This moment.

"I wouldn't say *scared*," he said. "I didn't want to mess this up. I don't think you get how big it was... to finally meet someone else like me. It was only me and my grandpa before, and when I saw you disappear, I nearly lost it. I wasn't alone anymore. I had no plans of letting you go after that."

My center tingled, and I had to look away from his gaze because he looked at me like I was everything, and I wasn't everything. But it would be a lie if I didn't admit to myself that being in Eilam's presence was the most wholesome thing in the universe.

It felt like there were invisible strings tying us together, and the farther we were apart, the more I felt unhinged.

He spoke again. "My problem is that even though I shouldn't, I believe that perfect moments can exist in time and space even if we're flawed."

"But perfect is a letdown. It doesn't really exist."

He shrugged. "I don't know, being around you makes that feel possible."

I bit my smile. "Seriously?"

He came a step closer, and I could tell he wanted to reach out to me, but he didn't. "I'm serious. Since the moment I saw you at Kesha's house, I felt my universe crashing and burning into a star. And you were that star, you were Halley's Comet. And if I missed the opportunity to speak to you—who knew if I'd be around for the next time someone like you came along? I'd have to wait years, lifetimes. Meeting you was pivotal. Do you get that? I almost didn't go to that party, but I did, and now I'm here, with *you*."

"So that makes *this* a perfect timeline?"

"Minus the part where I lied."

"And maybe the part where I yelled," I added. He didn't say anything, and I pressed the toe of my shoe into the concrete, a scraping sound. "I'm really sorry about that. And look, I forgive you, but you have to promise me. Promise me you'll never lie to me again, okay? I don't want secrets with you."

A smile again, but not because he was teasing. It was genuine. "I promise you."

I nodded, said, "Okay," and he smiled with all his teeth. I chewed my lip, walked to the passenger side. "Where to?"

"I hope you like pancakes," he said, and it just so happened, I did.

Very, very much.

THIRTY-THREE

The booth was cold and a little sticky when I slid into it.

Around us, music played through the speakers. It was midnight, and the only places open this late around here were IHOP and Waffle House. Eilam choose IHOP.

The waitress bore tired eyes as she slid two mugs in front of us and poured coffee into them before leaving the pot behind. I almost wanted to offer her the first sip. "I'll be back around in a little while. Let me know if y'all need anything else."

But there really wasn't anyone here. A few stragglers, sure, but I watched her return to the check-in area and hunch over the podium with a phone out in one hand, the other pressing into her cheek.

Eilam took a sip of his coffee, lips puckering as he set the mug back down.

"World's finest, huh?" I asked, picking up my own mug and having a sip. It wasn't the worst, but then again, I wasn't a barista at a hipster café. Eilam probably had the luxury of drinking the finest coffee on the daily.

I got a small smile from that comment, but I wanted more. "So, let's start over, 'kay?"

He pushed his eyebrows together. "Umm...okay."

"I'm Hylee Williams. I'm seventeen, and I go to Lee's Summit West. I want to be an illustrator, and I've been thinking about attending the Kansas City Art Institute. What about you?"

He took another sip, turned the mug on the table after, and then looked at me. "I'm Eilam Roads. I'm a barista, and I go to Grandview High School. I want to be an audio engineer, but I'm not sure what college I want to go to yet, or if I want to go far away or not. But I do know this: It is certainly nice to meet you, Hylee Williams."

I laughed a little. "So how do you do it?"

His head tilted to the side, his hands and elbows resting on the table. "What?"

"It," I said, trying not to say *time travel*, though I felt a little silly when I looked around again, remembering that we were essentially alone. But I needed to know.

His face brightened, brows raising. "Ah, yes. *It.* Do you want the technicalities or the dumbed-down version?"

"Try not to make the dumbed-down version sound so awful."

He smirked. Then the waitress came back. We placed our orders, and when she left, Eilam said, "Essentially, I focus on the time and place I want to be, and then I end up there."

"Wait. So all you have to do is focus?"

"Yeah, which is why I'm so intrigued by you. When it happened for me the first time, I was coincidentally thinking about one of my favorite memories as a child, and then I ended up there. It was my grandpa who trained me to keep my focus."

"Right, you did say your grandpa could travel, too. It's interesting. Can anyone else in your family?"

"Nope. It was me and him before he passed."

"Oh."

"But I can see him whenever I want." He pointed to his head. "Remember? I just have to focus on a time when we were together, and I'm there."

My mind raced, and I remembered the coin in my pocket. I always had it on me now, and maybe . . . maybe I could learn to focus. Go back to the dark place, see if Bubba was there. "And your mom knows?"

"Yeah, it was her dad who could time travel."

I was quiet. I couldn't believe that Eilam had grown up knowing that this could happen to him, and then it did happen to him, and when it did, he had support. People who helped him. People who didn't keep secrets. Now he sat across from me without any fear that he'd be grabbed by the wrist and taken somewhere else against his will.

"What about you? Anyone else in your family?"

Took another sip of coffee. "No." My voice cracked still. "At least, not that I know of."

"My grandpa used to tell me that it was genetically passed down. While we don't know the complete genealogy of it, he's told me that he came across someone else who had the same theories."

"Really? I guess that's . . . interesting. I can't think of anyone in my family, but there's a lot I don't know about our past. Can you also travel to alternate realities?"

His pinkish lips glistened, and I stared at them while he spoke. "No. Another interesting thing about you. I was actually serious when I said I'd only seen that in comics, but it's possible. I don't know how to access it, though."

The waitress returned with food. Strawberry banana pancakes for him and chocolate chip pancakes for me.

While we ate, I asked him more questions between each bite. I wanted to know everything he knew, and even though I didn't ask for it, he gave me the theories on why he believed people like us time traveled.

There was something comforting about this moment. Knowing he could relate to what I'd been going through made me feel like I had validity to hold on to.

More than that, there was this feeling I got when Eilam scrunched his face to the side, thinking, or when his eyes met mine with a smile—all of it pointing to an intimacy I'd felt somehow before.

Eilam offered to pay, and then by 1:00 a.m., we were out of there.

On the car ride to Grandmommy's, I kept looking at Eilam. I remembered how we had kissed. How we had shared the same breath, and I couldn't stop thinking about it. I didn't know when it would happen again, if I'd ruined that part, but I wanted it so badly.

When we parked, I wasn't ready to go in yet. "Wanna go on a walk with me?" I was a little nervous when I asked, because what if he was tired of hanging out with me?

"You don't want our date to end, do you?"

"Date?"

"This is a date. Part two of part one."

"What was part one?"

"When I picked you up from your parents' house like a gentleman and bought you pancakes. Part two is now."

I smiled, didn't say anything, and got out the car, rushing to the sidewalk that would take me away from Grandmommy's.

Eilam followed, locking his door, and I picked up the pace, giggling when I glanced back to see how he looked in the early morning. His curls ruffled, his eyes bright and wide, mouth open to catch his breath.

The sight of him created a beating so hard against my throat I had to swallow. Because when he slowed down and came closer to me, it was hard to breathe. I liked how we were this close. How he looked down at me with a smile that made me want to forget about everything else in the world.

Was it possible that he felt the same way?

"Will you show me your art sometime?"

His question threw me off. "Really?"

He nodded. "Yeah—you mentioned art back at IHOP, and I'd love to see it. I'm sure, knowing you, it's amazing."

I bit my lip. "Don't make me blush."

"Am I?"

I broke his stare and began to walk. "A little."

I heard him laugh, and then he took a few big steps to catch up to me.

"I post all my stuff on Tumblr. You can follow me there if you want."

"Cool. I will."

"But if you're looking at my stuff, I want to see your stuff, too. It has to be an even exchange."

"Right, because we're equals," he added.

"Exactly. Fuck the patriarchy."

Eilam stopped walking to make a face. It was a look of surprise and agreement, but he was silent far longer than I was comfortable with. "What?"

"Fuck the patriarchy," he said.

I grinned, and we started walking again. "We love a woke king."

He stuck his tongue out. "Not the biggest fan of that term."

"Ha. Me either. I just wanted to see you make that face."

"Tsk. Tsk. Did you know *patriarchy* literally means *the rule of the father*? That's enough alone to tell you how oppressive it is to women."

I made a yacking sound, and we took a few more strides before I said, "What else do you know about time travel?"

"I read somewhere that since the atoms that make up our bodies were once the core of a star that went supernova billions of years ago, you could theoretically argue that we're all time travelers.

Because if that star came to be when the universe did, then we're all connected to the beginning of time."

"You didn't see that from an Instagram post, did you?"

He laughed. "No, I actually read it in an article."

"Do you like science, Eilam?"

"I like making sense of what's happening around me."

"But what if you can't?"

He grabbed my hand, squeezed it, and we stopped walking.

Journeys end in lovers meeting.

"If I can't, then it's not the end of the world. That's why Grandpa told me to stay grounded. Hold on to what is real. It keeps you here," he said, looking at our hands connected. And I knew I wasn't going anywhere. Not now. Not while we touched.

"Can I try something?" His voice so low, the wind would have blown it away if I weren't already looking at his lips.

"Of course," I murmured.

"Hold on to me, okay?"

I nodded, and I stretched myself, wrapping my arms around his neck and resting my head against his chest. He held me, too. His palm pressed against my back. This was a forever feeling. He leaned to whisper in my ear. "Breathe with me, and I'll count. In and out."

"Okay," I said, and I took a deep breath in.

"One," he said.

Deep breath out.

"Two," he whispered, and I closed my eyes.

Deep breath in.

"Three," he said, but the end of his word was caught in something.

Suddenly, I felt like he lifted me up in one swift moment and then planted my feet firmly on the ground, a crunching sound beneath my shoes.

And the air was cold when I inhaled again, the frost icing my lungs. Opened my eyes to see snow falling in small flakes around us.

My gasp caught in my chest, and Eilam said, "It's okay. We did it."

We did it? I released my grip from him to see. Snow covered every surface. Thick white blankets coated the streets, the sidewalk we stood on, and the yards around us. We were in front of Eilam's house.

"It's Christmas morning, exactly six years ago. Look," he said, and he pointed to the window. Inside, I could see a family gathered around a colorful Christmas tree. "It was the last Christmas when my grandpa was alive."

I couldn't believe we were here. Couldn't believe that within three seconds we'd time traveled together and that this was the outcome.

"Keep looking," he said, still pointing to the window. "Watch."

I peered, my eyes narrowing, almost leaning forward. And then a Black man with a peppered beard and a Santa Claus hat looked up at us, and he waved.

I gasped. "How does he know?"

"I've been here before, and sometimes I come back to see him wave at me."

"How are there not multiples of you?" I looked around.

He shrugged. "I don't know. I thought there would be, but there hasn't been. My only thought is that I've reset something somehow, but I don't know what."

"Aren't you afraid?"

He shook his head. "No."

"Why?" I whispered, thinking the morning streets would share our secrets with everyone.

"Because I'm supposed to be here right now. Every time I come back, I'm supposed to. This is destiny, Hylee."

He wrapped me back in his arms. Three seconds later, we were back on the sidewalk in Grandmommy's neighborhood, the sky not as dark as it was before.

My arms were still locked around Eilam when we came back, and I didn't want to let him go. I turned to face him, bringing my nose to his nose.

Those images came rushing back. Me and Eilam holding hands. Eilam whispering in my ear. Me tackling him into a pile of freshly raked leaves. Eilam everywhere. All at once. All the time.

And I didn't want to let any of this go.

THIRTY-FOUR

Grandmommy was asleep when I snuck inside. It was almost four in the morning now.

Slipped my things onto the floor by the entryway and made a quick right into the dining room. This room was never used, but it was staged. Wooden table with fine porcelain set in front of each chair. Beautiful paintings and a rug more expensive than any of the items I had in my room.

Against the wall, across from the window, there was a pale blue sideboard with three drawers running across the top row. This piece was passed down to Grandmommy. Maybe it held some answers about Bubba and that night. I knew my dad trusted his mom with everything. She'd even held on to me and Bubba's birth certificates at one point because she didn't want them to get lost with all the moving.

Pulled a drawer open to find tea-light candles, a lighter, and glassware. The next one was similar to the first, but there was a letter opener, doilies, and some other cloth thing folded neatly. The last one held a few papers, but no papers I was looking for.

Where else could Grandmommy be hiding things? There had to be something.

In the dim light, the shadows pouring in from the window, it hit me. Downstairs, to the right of that old desk that was never used, was a two-tier file cabinet. Secrets were always kept behind locks.

Sprinted up the staircase to my bathroom. Found a bobby pin and ran back down, taking two steps at a time as my heart throbbed in my throat and I almost tripped.

Downstairs, I flipped on the single light, and the coldness from the concrete walls brought goose bumps to my arms and shoulders. My fingers traced the wooden desk, picking up dust, particles glistening.

There, the metal file cabinet sat sandwiched between this desk and the wall. Bent down to see it at eye level. Tried a drawer, just in case. Locked, as I figured. But this old thing, it wanted to be opened, didn't it?

Folded my lip as I stared it down, placing a palm against it. *Just please open, okay?*

The silver lock was in the top corner, and I bit off the small bulbs at the end of the bobby pin before placing it in the lock. Pressed my ear against the drawer, the cold cooling my cheek. Was this how it worked? I thought I'd seen something like this in a movie before.

I could hear the mechanics, and then the bobby pin hit a small thunk. Something else metal. I wiggled it gently, turned it to the right, and then I felt it: a release.

This time, with the bobby pin still turned, I pulled on the top drawer, and it opened. There was a stale paper smell from inside, and the file folders were labeled in blue ink from *A* to *Z*.

In the first file, there was a small folded paper—a receipt to something. Maybe a small business she used to donate to or was affiliated with?

The next folder had a small green pouch. I pulled it out to open it. Inside were three small rectangular pieces of paper. The first one was Daddy's birth certificate.

Name: Lawrence Eugene Williams
Birth date: December 8, 1976
Birth time: 11:59 p.m.
Hospital: Bethany Medical Center

County: Wyandotte

City: Kansas City

State: Kansas

Mother: Lorraine Mabel Williams

Father: Blank

Behind it was Grandmommy's birth certificate:

Name: Lorraine Mabel Williams

Birth date: April 16, 1954

Birth time: 2:18 p.m.

Hospital: Graham County Hospital

County: Graham

City: Hill City

State: Kansas

Mother: Alice Mae Williams

Father: Otis Michael Williams

And last, another birth certificate. I hoped maybe it was Bubba's because if it were, then it meant there could be more here, hidden.

Name: Atticus Joel Williams

Birth date: September 14, 1971

Birth time: 5:45 p.m.

Hospital: Graham County Hospital
County: Graham
City: Hill City
State: Kansas
Mother: Lorraine Mabel Williams
Father: Blank

As soon as I gasped, a light turned on. I almost didn't notice, because apparently five years before Daddy was born, there was an Atticus, born in the same city that Grandmommy grew up in. Daddy had a brother? But how? Grandmommy said she'd only had Daddy, that the doctors said she couldn't really have kids.

But then Grandmommy came whipping around the corner, robe flapping from the breeze she conjured. "What in heaven's name are you doing down here?"

THIRTY-FIVE

A brown braid rested on Grandmommy's shoulder, and a satin scarf was tied neatly to the top of her head. Her lips tight, robe undone, arms pressing to her side.

Well, it was her face that said it, not her lips. The way her brows were raised, and she leaned in, chin pointing toward me, her eyes bolting to the bobby pin sticking out of the lock. She'd probably never trust me again, but what else was I supposed to do?

I didn't know what to say. What could I? I was busted. But beside that, there was this. This secret. And I didn't know what it meant, but it had to be something. Why was she hiding it?

"Grandmommy, what is this?"

She snatched the bag out of my hand, the papers, too. I flinched, blinking as she moved.

"What are you even doing here? Aren't you supposed to be with your parents?"

She was deflecting, but I was tired of the shit. "You had another son?"

Her mouth parted, and she shifted her weight from foot to foot.

"Atticus?" I said, and I watched her place the papers back in the pouch and zip it.

"I'm disappointed in you, Hylee."

"You're disappointed in me? I'm not the one hiding secrets!"

"Don't." She raised a finger. "Don't you dare raise your voice. Not in my house."

I huffed, pressing myself further into the hard floor. "What happened to him?"

She tried to swallow the lump in her throat, but the words came out with a sharpness anyway. "It . . . it is rude to go through other people's personal things, Hylee."

"Does Daddy know?"

"No, and I would like to keep it that way."

"Is he still in Graham County?"

Her eyes low, tucking the green pouch beneath her arm. "He is."

I felt my chest rise. I had an uncle. "So why haven't we met him? What's the surprise?"

"There is no surprise. He is dead, Hylee, and that is all you need to know. Go to bed." She turned with one quick pivot, switching off the lights and leaving the basement.

I felt each creak as she walked up the steps, leaving me with my knees pressed into the thin rug in the dark. How could I sleep with that kind of news? How could anyone sleep?

And he was dead? How? What happened to him and when? Maybe it was recent, and he'd been living in Graham County this entire time? But that wouldn't explain why Grandmommy would keep him from us. So then, maybe he died a long time ago? But how?

My eyes darted in the darkness, and alone I started to see flashes of the dark place. It wasn't real here, but I wasn't so sure anymore.

The shadows grew ferociously, falling through the cracks somehow. I could hear the vines bursting from the ground, slithering on the floor. A breeze from nowhere. The smell of wet, rich soil, and the sound of something skittering across the floor.

The shadows were following me, but the sudden surprise made me time travel, too.

In the dark place, I was on my feet, in the middle of my

childhood bedroom as I came to. My center of gravity felt like it shifted, dizziness setting in, and I almost hurled.

It was the thudding of the wood that shook me into realization.

Flinched. Looked at the clock. 9:10 p.m. And right in front of me, the girl. Me. *Us.*

She went for the doorknob before I could get to it, and I chased after her, hearing the yelling again. The voice was so distorted, it was hard to tell if it was my dad.

Regardless, it was a warning that made me pause, and if I knew better, if I *knew* what was good for me, I'd listen to that. I'd stay right here, planted. But the light from the hallway drew me in. Bubba could be here, and if he was, I needed to see him. I'd waited too long for that. And I had to know what had happened. This could be my only chance.

Took a step forward. A gun was fired. Then footsteps. Someone running. A door being slammed, and I jumped as I crept forward. My skin cold, my fingers trembling.

"Hylee!" someone yelled. And I knew that voice. I *knew* that voice. I'd carried it in my heart for nine years because I never wanted to forget it. I never wanted to forget *him.*

And now? Now I could not wait. Little Hylee and I opened the door, and I hurried to the hallway, past the younger version of me. My hip smashed into the door frame as I made it out. *Bubba.* It was all I could think. The only thing pulling me forward.

He was here. He was close.

The narrow hallway, the pale yellow walls. Ruins now. Darkness crawling from corners, dirt and vines twisting in cracks. And then three things happened.

First, Hylee.

She stood toward the end of the hall. I could only make out part of her face, but she seemed afraid. And not a single second of this was familiar to me.

Second, my dad.

He, thorns running down his arms, hands held up in surprise, rushed in from the kitchen. Beside him, coming into the hallway at full throttle, my brother. Bubba. He wasn't how I remembered him, either. Lips twisting through his face. Leaves sewn in his hair. Eyes gone. Then the sound of a gun being fired again, and Bubba reached out to little Hylee, trying to scoop her into his arms as a bullet flew toward him, piercing him somewhere as he fell into the younger me, and they both disappeared. Gone.

I . . . I freaking time traveled, and wherever I went, Bubba went there, too.

My dad also disappeared, but not how Hylee and Bubba had; he'd run because the man with the mask and the gun was coming toward him.

And then, third.

Rushing in from the living room, after the man, after the gunshot, was *Bubba*.

Not the Bubba who had just disappeared, but *my* Bubba. Tall, chest heaving, his brown face pale. And he was human, like me. Like he didn't belong here. *How?*

As I pressed my palms to my mouth to gasp, his eyes snapped in my direction, his lips parting at the sight of me. The surprise closed in on both of us.

He was here. He was here. He was here. *Alive.*

The moment we stretched for each other, I disappeared, my own reality pulling me back from this twisted timeline.

THIRTY-SIX

PRESENT DAY: MARCH

I reappeared in the pitch-black basement, and I hurried up the stairs. It was almost six in the morning. That was the longest I'd ever been gone.

But Bubba, he was alive. It was his voice I kept hearing in my head like some omen. That was him. Had *always* been him.

I needed to know how to get back to Bubba—how to control what was happening to me—and the only person I knew who had the ability to do that was Eilam. I needed him to show me everything.

I texted Eilam, my thumbs moving so fast, I wasn't sure if any of what I said made sense; I just wanted to make sure he knew.

I kicked off my shoes when I got to my bedroom, flipped on my lamp. I had to draw Bubba how I saw him because he was alive, and oh my god, I couldn't believe he was alive. And I didn't know if anyone would believe me; I just knew that I couldn't forget this.

My playlist rotated to a new song as the sun pierced the horizon. I could see the sunlight stretching to my window, illuminating parts of my desk. I tweaked his nose one last time, and I dated the bottom right corner of it.

It was my brother. His face centered on this piece of paper, his expression equally confused and surprised.

"I'm going to come back for you," I whispered to the paper.

And I left it there, on my desk, so that the sunlight would draw itself in it, too.

After I washed up, I climbed into bed, and I slept hard. My dreams were on repeat of me in the dark place, running down the hall, seeing my brother at the end of it. And behind him, my grandmother, holding a baby wrapped in a blanket. Because there was Atticus. She'd had another son, and she'd kept it a secret from all of us, and I still didn't know why.

I'd fallen asleep with my phone in my hand, and it was the vibration that woke me up. It was Eilam, video calling me.

"Are you okay? Is everything okay?"

I sat up, rubbed my eyes. "Are you free? Can we hang?" I said, my mouth tasting like sleep. He looked tired, too. His face puffy.

"Yeah, I can pick you up. Be there in thirty."

I rushed to get dressed, and before I knew it, Eilam was texting to say he was here. The moment I closed the car door, he asked if everything was okay again, and I explained what happened. What I remembered from the incident. The information I'd found out about my uncle, and then how I returned to the dark place and saw my brother.

He looked speechless. He rubbed his chin, and he started a few sentences but stopped them. "I'm sorry about what happened to your family. Wow, it's . . . it's a lot. How do you feel about all of this?"

"I don't know," I said, and he looked like he wanted to hug me. "I just know that I need to get back there."

"You sure it was really him?"

"Yeah, I've never been more certain."

"Didn't you say that the people . . . they looked like monsters?"

"But he wasn't. I swear. He looked like you and me. And he recognized me. I remember you mentioned how time travel is about focusing, and I need you to show me how. Can you?"

He nodded, and when we got to his house, it was empty. His mom was at work; Julius was with his dad.

"Want anything to drink? Want me to make you some coffee?"

I shook my head. I could feel the heaviness under my eyes, but this was the only thing I wanted to focus on right now.

I got on the floor, my head pressing against the carpet in the living room.

Eilam laughed. "You sure you don't want coffee?"

I smiled. "I'm not about to fall asleep." I patted the ground beside me. "Can you show me?"

He looked at me for a long while, pressed a thumb to my arm. "I can't believe I'm doing this."

I sat up. "What? Did I say something wrong?"

"No. It's déjà vu. Being here with you, doing this. I never thought I'd do something like this. I'm just wondering if Grandpa felt the same way."

"What was it like for you when you were learning?"

"Hard." He chuckled, and I squinted. "I feel like that came out wrong."

"Sure." I smiled. "But really, how was it?"

"I mean it really was difficult. Grandpa gave me small tasks until we worked up to big ones. At first it was time traveling to five minutes ago, and then it was meeting him at a park he'd taken me to a week prior. So with you—with us doing this all at once—I'm not certain what the outcome will look like . . . but we can still try."

I nodded.

"My grandpa said the best way to make time travel happen was to be spectacular at focusing. So here—" He motioned for me to lie down, and I did. Then Eilam placed one hand on my stomach and the other on my chest. "Is this okay?"

I felt my chest get warm; my stomach tightened. It wasn't too long ago when we were stomach-to-stomach on his bed, laughing between kisses, and even now, looking at his lips made me want to reach my hand to his neck, lower him down to me.

"Yeah. This is fine," I said, trying to keep my cool. *Focus.* I needed to focus.

"Now every time you breathe, you'll feel it in both places," he said, and then he picked up my hands, placed one on my chest, and the other on my stomach. "There."

Eilam lay beside me then, and he closed his eyes, breathing in through his nostrils and out through his mouth. He kept doing it, so I mimicked him. After a few minutes we were deep breaths and warm air.

Eilam whispered, "How do you feel?"

I took another breath, both my hands rising and falling. "Maybe like I could fly."

"Do you feel any tingling?"

I surveyed my limbs. "No."

"Hm, okay. Let's have you focus on where it is you want to go."

"'Kay," I breathed, and I thought of the hallway in my old home over and over again. I thought of Bubba's face. I tried to remember what used to be on the walls in the hallway, but all I really remembered were the holes and crumbling paint from the dark place. The shadows inhabited every corner, stretching like cobwebs.

But there was a door in the hallway. What color was that door? Brown, maybe? Or white? It could be white. And off that hallway? My old bedroom, and then another room. My parents' room.

As I continued to try to pull together the pieces of the hallway, my feet began to tingle, and the feeling crept to my ankles, and then to my knees. My stomach turned a little, my eyes twitch. And then, for the tiniest second, I was there. On the rug . . . or maybe it was hardwood floors? It was only a second, and I felt my cells breathe me in, but when I opened my eyes, I was at Eilam's still, and he was propped up.

"You glitched."

My ears were warm. "I thought I was there. I could almost feel it."

"Glitching is part of the process."

I pinched my fingers into the carpet. I didn't want to glitch. I just wanted to be there. I wanted to talk to my brother.

Eilam noticed my mood shift.

"Hey . . . hey, it's a process, okay? You've got this. Let's try again." He lay back down, and I followed suit. "Try visualizing yourself in that exact same moment again. But don't just think about your brother, okay? Think about the whole house. Sometimes we have to widen our perspective, shake up our memory. The synapses in our bodies are like jumper cables—we've got to give them something to connect to so we can land in the moments we want."

I whispered, "Okay." Closed my eyes, and I thought of the hallway again. Bubba stood at the end of it, at the entryway to the living room.

What was the living room like? Hardwood floors. Walls covered in pictures, and two couches. A coffee table. A lamp. But the rest . . . the rest of the house slipped away.

The tingling came back, some of it in the tips of my fingers now. This time, I heard Bubba say my name. I didn't know what else was said; just that I heard it. And I could almost feel myself there again, could hear the heat kick on to warm the house.

More tingling.

More feeling like I was going to zap away, but . . . I didn't end up going anywhere.

After a while, I opened my eyes, and Eilam was looking at me again.

"Why does this keep happening?"

"It's hard. You're working a muscle you didn't even know you had."

I sighed.

"My grandpa said that sometimes retracing your steps can help visualize better. Do you have any photo albums you can look at?"

"No." Then I chewed my lip, remembering that my childhood home now sat empty in the neighborhood. "But what are the chances that I can convince you to go on an adventure with me?"

"Depends on what kind of trouble you're trying to get me into?"

I smiled, showing all my teeth. "No trouble. Just a little breaking and entering, is all."

THIRTY-SEVEN

When we turned onto my old street, my stomach tightened like a fist.

We crept up a hill, made it to a stop, and as we rode down it, I felt the swelling in my chest.

In my mind, I kept thinking someone else lived here now, a new family. Three kids. A mom and dad who were protective, but not too hovering. A loyal dog, and two rescue cats. I'd imagine that they'd have a garden in the backyard, a revamped sitting area in the gazebo, and that somehow they'd finally get grass to grow by the sidewalk in the front yard. They'd protect the home with an animalistic urgency, so hungry to keep everything and everyone safe because this would be the haven they'd have many firsts in— whether good or bad.

There wasn't any of that.

Instead, we pulled into the front of the driveway, and Eilam put the car in park but kept the engine running, as if he were asking if I were sure.

But I couldn't pull my gaze away from it. Past the tree in the front, there the house sat. Could a house breathe? This one felt like it could—like it had exhaled so madly that it caused the brown shingles to split and crack.

The wooden fence around the perimeter of the house, my old house, was half painted, half tagged with graffiti, and half leaning. The cast-iron fence with the points at the end of the driveway—gone. Vines twisted themselves around the hatching of the gazebo, and bright green weeds pushed themselves through parts of the driveway. The grass was overgrown, and this place looked like it could have been hidden in the woods.

It had been nine years since my family lived here, but I refused to believe we were the last. There were those small changes I could point out, tell you what had been here before and what hadn't. But I wondered if our past trauma stuck to the walls, and maybe it was that, the haunting of our screams and cries, that pushed out whoever lived here after us. *The Afters.*

"Will you keep lookout?" I said, opening the door.

Eilam looked around. "You want me to just sit out here with the car running?"

"I guess you could walk if you wanted to."

He chuckled nervously. "Nah, that's okay. I'll be here if you need me." He grabbed my hand before I got out. "You sure you don't want me to go in with you?" There was a flicker in his brown eyes, a small smile painted on his face.

I shook my head. "I think it's best if I do this one alone."

I walked down the driveway, passing windows on the side of the house that I knew connected to bedrooms. My parents' had been there, my brother's up there, and around the corner, here, was mine.

My first thought was to try the window, but when it didn't open, I ventured farther around the house to the garage. The birds sang somewhere in the distance, and I looked to my left and my right.

There was a chance—regardless of how small—that someone *could* be living here. If that were the case, what I was doing would absolutely be classified as breaking and entering, and if I got caught, Grandmommy would kill me.

The trees rustled, and I tried my hand at the window, pushing up with all my might until I heard a crack and a release, paint splitting at the corners and particles flying around me.

I opened it the rest of the way, and I pressed the toe of my Nikes into the siding, hiked up the wall, placing one foot through the window and climbing in until I landed on a concrete floor. The garage had two windows, and they lit the space well enough that I could see everything I needed to. There were some old newspapers on the floor, a box in the corner, and plenty of dust and grime.

Daddy used to park his truck in here, and Bubba and I would get in the car and pretend like we were going on a road trip. We'd even bring our blankets in and take fake naps while we took turns driving.

And above me, that small cutout there, that led to the storage space where Mama and Daddy kept the Christmas tree. That Christmas—the last one we had here—I'd climbed up to the attic and helped Bubba get it down, old webs getting stuck in my curls and eyelashes. He'd laughed, called me a witch, and when I saw myself in the mirror, I'd laughed, too.

Directly in front of me was a door. It led to the inside of the house, but when I tried the knob, it was locked. I'd suspected this could happen. I pulled my crossbody bag to the front of me, unzipped the small zipper, and pulled out a butter knife.

Again, breaking and entering.

Again, Grandmommy would kill me, but this was a chance for me to really remember—a chance to experience this home one last time and figure out what happened the night my brother disappeared. Whatever the risk, this was worth it.

It was Bubba who taught me this. You'd wedge the knife between the frame and the little latch that locked the door in place. I was five when I locked myself in the bathroom. I remembered crying so hard, thinking I'd be stuck in there for the rest of my life.

"You have to wiggle it like this," Bubba had said, moving the knife back and forth between the door and the frame. I could hear the wood splitting, and then the door popped open like magic. We smiled at each other then, and I swear to you, my brother was so damn cool. He gave me a hug.

"Don't worry. I won't tell Mama or Daddy," he'd said.

Now I did just as he told me, getting the door unlocked. I made it look easier than it was, but that was because I'd gotten plenty of practice in the last few years: waking Mama and Daddy up so they made it to work on time, getting Mama out of the closet after a drunken fiasco, getting a cousin out (who'd also accidentally locked themselves inside), and snooping. I couldn't help myself.

I stood in the dining room now. A window with broken blinds to my left, and a door that was blocked with a wooden bar beside it. I remembered that door. I remembered we'd never, ever used it. I never knew why, but it was still boarded off today.

This room used to have a brown dining room table with matching chairs—plastic still on the part where you placed your butt because it was white, and Mama didn't want our little fingers to get sauce all over it. We never really used that room, anyway.

And there used to be tall buffets that held Mama and Daddy's fancy plates and glassware. Stuff from their wedding. Items inherited and passed down. Things we never ate off of, and never touched. A small twinge inside me, knowing full well that all those things went in a dump once the bank took the house back. If we'd known then what we knew now, I wondered if—for once—Mama would have let us eat a meal on those fancy plates.

Today, this room had a few crunchy leaves on the wooden floor, debris and dust, and nothing else. To my left, the back door that led to the porch, and in front of me, two steps that led to the kitchen.

The kitchen was different than I remembered. The brown cabinets were now white. The floors didn't have the peeling stuff that we used to have—now they were wooden, and I wondered if they had always been here the whole time.

I couldn't remember the last meal we ate in here, but I remembered Mama spent so much time in the kitchen. Not just to cook, but it was where she hung out with her friends. She'd do hair in the kitchen. She'd write down grocery lists and talk on the phone about awful customers she'd had to deal with. She'd paint her nails at the table that was in here, and I'd join her, painting my toes to match.

Our ghosts were here, breathing through the walls. Could the house really belong to anyone else when it felt like it still belonged to us?

There were two exits off the kitchen, an opening to the living room and an opening to a hallway (which also opened to the living room).

As I considered which path to take, a flash of a memory hit me hard. Me chasing Bubba, round and round. Our exhausted breaths and giggles vibrating through the floor. Mama yelling at us to stop running. Me, with an old baby doll in hand, trying to force Bubba to kiss it.

I entered the living room, my stomach tight. Our older cousin died here. *Boom. Boom.* The gunshots. Killing Juice immediately. The blood soaked the rug that used to be in here, and now there was beige carpet. A new front door, since the old one had been kicked in. The same windows, and memories of me and Bubba pressing our noses to them, watching a blizzard fill the Kansas streets.

Flashes of blood and darkness. My knees wobbled. I held my frame against the wall next to me. Deep breaths in, deep breaths out. And I pleaded with my body not to take me, but it was just a bad memory. No time traveling. Not yet. I wanted to go on my own terms.

"Bubba, I'm coming for you," I whispered to the empty living room.

My fingers traced the wall as I moved to the hallway. The hallway. The last time I'd seen Bubba alive. The first time I'd been taken to the dark place. All of it here, in this narrow, dark space.

Pulled out my phone, turned on the flashlight. A creak, and my heart skipped a beat. It was just the wooden floor.

I flashed my light on the doors. There were three in front of me, all closed. The bathroom door, and two bedrooms. One that had belonged to me, and one that had belonged to my parents.

Behind me, the basement door. And it was wooden and white. All of them were white. This was the hallway, and I needed to remember every moment of it because I needed my memory to take me back to that day, so I could get Bubba and bring him back with me. I took pictures of it—literally and mentally. I wanted to sketch this out later.

Of all the doors, I chose to enter my old bedroom.

Turned the knob with a held breath, and more filtered sunlight met me where I was. It smelled like something old and sitting.

I pressed my palm against the walls in here, sweeping past what was once my very first canvas. I'd never forget the time I'd gotten in trouble for drawing life-sized flowers with crayons and markers. Mama bought me my first drawing pad after that, said, *You draw on papers, not on walls.*

I remembered, behind my bedroom door, Bubba and I had set up a science experiment. We wanted to know if we took an egg from the fridge, kept it warm, would it hatch into a baby chick? We took one of my old teddy bears, placed an egg in its arms (because the baby chick would need a mom), and we set it behind the door, next to the warm vent. Days went by. A chick never hatched, but we eventually found yellow gunk covering the teddy bear.

I leaned against the window that overlooked the back porch, and I slid to the floor, pressed my knees to my chest, and closed my eyes.

Tried to remember all of it. All the times I convinced Bubba to play Barbies with me. All the movies we watched in a fort we'd made. All the times I'd hidden under my bed, in the closet, or behind a dresser.

I remembered our family movie nights, all four of us full of pizza, squished on a couch, watching the big-screen TV. Mama always fell asleep, and we'd laugh, and Daddy would take pictures and show them to her the next day. I remembered all the parties my family had here. The loud bass, and the people congregating everywhere. Daddy used to be the life of the party. We used to have it all.

I opened my eyes, and none of that was here. It hadn't been for almost a decade. Then I crossed my legs, my hands on my knees, and I tried to narrow in on time and space.

The plan was never to time travel from in the house... but I was here now, fingertips pressing into my dark blue jeans, legs and thighs squishing into the cold carpet. Back against the wall—inhaling, feeling my chest rise and fill. Exhaling—feeling the air leave my body. I had to do it now because what if—*what if I can't when I'm away from this place?*

Everything I needed was right here.

Took another deep breath in and deep breath out. I pictured this room I was in, how it looked in the dark place. The shadows spreading like ink in water.

Focus, I told myself. *Focus.*

The world seemed so quiet after that. I wanted to be there. I whispered that to myself like a chant. I wanted it to be the only thing I focused on. There was a small shift, some tingling in my ankles, a smell different than the place that surrounded me.

And then the horn honked. I jumped, almost.

Shit.

That was it. It was my shot to try to get back to Bubba, and it was all over now. I'd failed again, and it didn't feel like I'd ever get a grip on this whole time traveling thing.

THIRTY-EIGHT

I climbed into my bed when I got back to Grandmommy's. Not hungry, the sun still in the sky, almost about to slip away.

If I wasn't so pissy, I'd stomp back downstairs and demand Grandmommy tell me what happened with Atticus.

Though she wouldn't want anything demanded of her—because that wasn't respectful—regardless, she wouldn't give in anyway. It would be on her terms. Something she made obvious as I walked in, and she refused to look in my direction.

She noted that I should consider calling my parents. That they deserved to know why I'd left the other day. I'd hate to admit it out loud, but she was right, and so as I pressed onward to my room, I texted my parents to tell them that I loved them, and that I was sorry for dipping so suddenly.

Maybe they'd text me back.

And now I lay in my bed feeling hopeless with my feet dangling off the side. I didn't want lies or secrets anymore; I wanted the truth.

I really thought being at that house would give me some kind of superhero power and launch me into whatever dimension I wanted to be in. But I wasn't an Avenger—I was just Hylee from Kansas City who missed her brother and who felt betrayed by her family. And I wanted to change that sentence so much. I wanted to be *Hylee who has a brother and lives in Kansas City with her loving family.*

Anyway, there was no promise that time traveling could make people change.

But . . . if I could get to the dark place, figure out why Bubba was there—why this realm had a hold on me—maybe I'd feel some relief. I could at least try.

Eilam said I needed to focus on my breathing, feel the air enter and leave my body.

I turned onto my back, placing a hand on my stomach and my

chest as he had earlier. Closed my eyes and focused on the sound of the house. I could hear the mumbles from the TV a floor below me. The beeping of the microwave. A car zooming past outside.

And I thought about Bubba; I thought about seeing him on November 9.

We were in our family home.

I was in my room.

I was making my bed.

As the thought came to, a wave of nausea rushed over me. Small chills ran from my shoulders to my feet. I blinked, and I could see it—could see my old room, could see my younger self throwing a pillow on the bed, could hear a bang.

But when I blinked again, I was back here.

I jumped out of bed and kicked it so hard, I hurt my toe. I crumpled onto the floor and screamed into my hands until tears stung at my eyes. I needed this. *Please just let me have this.*

I let another scream rip out of me, muffling it with my arm. When I calmed down, I forced myself to try again.

Breathe, Hylee. You've got this, I said to myself, and I had to believe it.

Another deep breath.

Another rise and fall.

The sound of my breathing vibrated around me, pressing me farther into the carpet. This time, I tried to visualize each moment like a line on paper, creating a shape that would eventually turn into a person or a landscape.

It was almost unsettling how I could hear the charcoal pressing into my drawing pad as I visualized the past, my memory sketching it out for me.

November 9.

There was a loud sound. Daddy had yelled. Bubba had called out for me. Mama had gone somewhere.

When I inhaled again, a slight breeze tickled my nose, and when I opened my eyes, the world tilted slowly around me. I was on my feet now, back in my childhood bedroom, the door open. The difference was that there were no vines. No dirt. No dark shadows pouring from the corners and crawling to the edge of the trim. It looked normal.

"Hylee!"

It was Bubba's voice. I ran to the hallway and the man with the mask shot at him as he ran to me, the *younger* version of me. He wrapped his arms around her, and they both disappeared. Just as I had seen in the dark place. But he wasn't a monster, and she wasn't a monster.

So then . . . *where was I?*

I heard the sound of metal clicking. A gun.

And Daddy, he was there, at the end of the hallway staring me down. *Me,* with bloodshot eyes so wide and confused. He didn't know who I was, but maybe he felt like he should know, that my face looked identical to his wife, to his daughter.

Except, the last time I'd seen this scene play out, I was in the dark place and Daddy didn't see me. He ran because Latrell had chased him down.

But the more I looked, the more I realized this wasn't the dark place. The way Daddy looked at me made me think I'd successfully time traveled to the past, but I didn't mean to end up here, I meant to go *there*, to find Bubba.

And if Daddy was supposed to run . . . a shot was fired. It was loud and then it hit something. Was this real or was I dreaming?

I heard a groan, and then Latrell appeared in the hallway. He was dressed in black from head to toe. A gun in hand. He pointed his gun toward me, and I ducked as he pulled the trigger. The sound so loud, my ears rang. I stumbled quickly into my bedroom, my hands shaking as I locked the door. This was real. This was not a dream.

A thud against the door, and I jumped. He was kicking at it from the other side.

I ran into the closet and tucked myself into the farthest part, stepping on a toy.

Closed my eyes and tried to breathe.

Grandmommy's house. My bedroom there. March 18.

Breathe. Breathe. Breathe.

A blow and the sound of the door being torn from its hinges. I could hear the wood crack and break.

Count to three, Hylee.

One.

I heard him shuffling through my room.

Two.

I heard him toss the mattress on my bed.

Three.

He headed for the closet, but then another breath, and I was gone.

I landed, lights bright in my eyes, and a scream. When I came to, Grandmommy was wrapped in her robe, eyes wide and saying, "Hylee! What—what are you doing here? You're supposed to be with your mom!"

THIRTY-NINE

I sat up, my head throbbing.

Grandmommy rushed to me, her eyes wild, a hand on my shoulder. "Did you hear me? How'd you get here?"

I blinked at her a few times, trying to piece her words together. What was she talking about? "Grandmommy, what do you mean?"

Her eyes darted back and forth as she stared at me. Then she got to her knees, took my hand and held it in hers. "Oh Lord, it's getting worse, isn't it?" She said it low, so low I almost missed it.

"You ... I. Yesterday, I dropped you off to spend time with your mom. Do you remember that?"

I shook my head slowly.

"You're here ... in Lee's Summit. You live with me, but school's out for spring break, and your mom missed you, and she wanted you to see her new apartment. She called me just after dinner last night to say that y'all had a good time—don't you remember that, sweetie?"

"Grandmommy—what? New apartment? When did my parents move? Wait ... why did my mom move? She has her own apartment now?"

She clicked her tongue, looked away from me, and her hands trembled in mine. I stared at them for a second, and then looked back at her hazel eyes. *Daddy*, I thought. *Daddy's eyes*. Did my parents split up? How had they not told me that?

I sighed, so confused. "What's going on?"

The rims of her eyes were red, her hair frazzled around her. "You don't remember, do you?" And I felt my face warming at how vague she was being. But I waited, wanted her to say more.

"What's the last thing you can recall?" she asked.

I squinted, trying to piece together the last two days. "I was with my parents, but I left, and when I came back here, I got caught snooping through your things—which, sorry—and you were upset that I found out about Atticus. After that ... um, I went to hang out with a friend, and then I came back here. I was in my room upstairs until..." I faltered because her eyes only got wider the more I spoke.

Did something awful happen after I left my parents' house the other day? Did someone break in again? Was that how this happened? Did they have to get an emergency apartment? My dad was too nice for his own good. I wouldn't be surprised if he'd invited a stranger in and they turned on him. I should have stayed.

Grandmommy shook her head rapidly, backed away. "You know about Atticus?"

"Yeah—you..." I stood up. "Don't you remember? I found his birth certificate. It said he was born in Hill City, like you. But... but you said he died, and then you were upset after."

Grandmommy stood, too. "Hylee, listen to me. What you're saying—none of that happened, okay?"

"Wait, Atticus isn't dead?"

She took a step closer. "No, Atticus...he is, but what you're saying. The course of events. None of that happened. And you shouldn't—you shouldn't know about him. I don't know what's going on, but I think it has something to do with you slipping away sometimes. That's why your mama sent you to live with me in the first place. You scared her, sweetie. Once the disappearing started happening, you kept asking about your brother and your dad, and it was too much for your mom to handle."

"But what happened with my dad—I'm so confused. What are you saying?"

"Hylee, your dad. He's been gone for a very long time. He died in that house—the night of the accident."

I gasped. "What?"

"I'm so, so sorry, honey. Everything that happened down there, it's all so unfortunate. I can't believe . . . you don't remember."

My voice cracked. "No, no, no. This isn't real. I must've messed something up." I stood up, paced frantically. I'd just seen my dad. He was alive and real. And when I time traveled . . . did *I* do this?

I dashed upstairs, Grandmommy calling after me. The room was different, drawings of my dad and my brother taped up by the desk, and multiple sketches of the dark place plastered everywhere.

I found my phone in my pocket, searching for my dad's contact but not finding it. How was this real, and what else had changed?

My fingers rushed as I typed Eilam's name into the search bar— when it appeared, I saw that we'd been texting almost every day. We knew each other still.

I called him immediately, my breath short as I tried to inhale as much air as I could. It felt like I might pass out.

He answered, and I hurried to talk. "Eilam. I need your help. Is there any way you can take me to see your grandpa?"

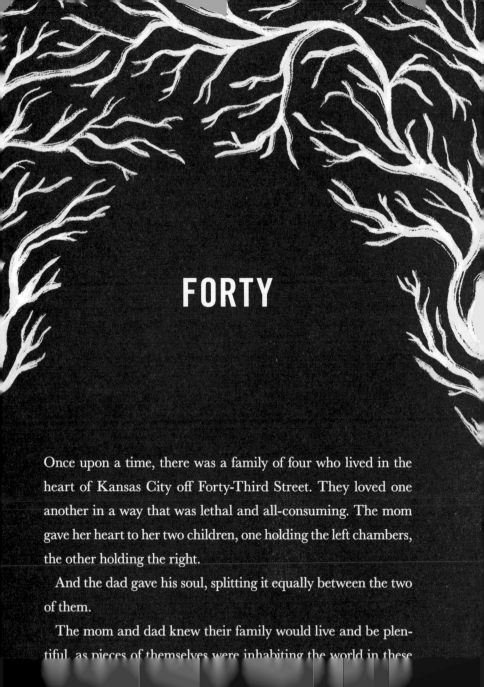

FORTY

Once upon a time, there was a family of four who lived in the heart of Kansas City off Forty-Third Street. They loved one another in a way that was lethal and all-consuming. The mom gave her heart to her two children, one holding the left chambers, the other holding the right.

And the dad gave his soul, splitting it equally between the two of them.

The mom and dad knew their family would live and be plentiful, as pieces of themselves were inhabiting the world in these

Together they could do it all, withstand any storm.

And so the four of them piled onto a three-seat couch, snuggling under a blanket. The sister settled beneath her dad's heart, his golden chain draped around her, and the brother was right against his mama, head on her shoulder, all of them connected. Forever, the four of them. Forever, the fantastic...

But then the world hid the brother, turning their lives upside down.

And the skies sent a cloud to swallow the sister, forcing them into disarray.

The mother's heart broke, and the dad lost his soul.

And their forever didn't feel so long anymore.

It was an empty couch, cold and alone in a house covered in soot and vines and leaves.

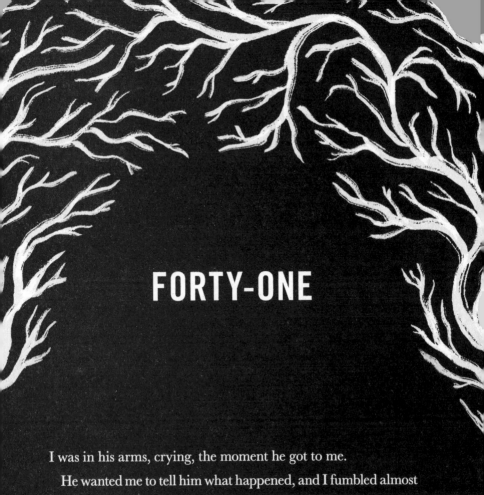

FORTY-ONE

I was in his arms, crying, the moment he got to me.

He wanted me to tell him what happened, and I fumbled almost every sentence that came out of my mouth until it was clear: I'd messed up the timeline.

Eilam told me that we met at Kesha's party, that I disappeared in front of him, that he'd hid his secret from me, that we'd fought. Everything he said made me believe that what changed in my life happened prior to moving in with Grandmommy, but after that, the sequence of who I met, the school I went to, was all the same.

But I needed clarity on how the world of time traveling worked.

and I needed it rather quickly if I wanted to get control of it—if I wanted to undo my father's death and save Bubba.

Eilam held my hand and took a breath. We were at his house in the living room.

"Are you sure it's okay for me to go with you? It won't ruin anything, right?"

He twisted his lips. "I think there's a good chance this could work out okay."

Chance? I needed more than that. "Can I ask, how do you know?"

"For starters, my grandfather is a genius. Second to that, right as he was beginning to get sick, he made a time travel landmark, which is basically like a landing place that's safe to travel to without having an effect on the current timeline. It was like when we time traveled to Christmas and saw my family, remember that?"

I nodded.

"When we did that, we didn't do anything that would change the outcome of the present. It'll essentially be the same thing."

"And where will we go this time?"

"What can I say? My grandpa is a big fan of the library, so we're gonna visit him there. On August 25, four years ago, he visited the downtown library in KC and checked out a room for himself. He told me the room was reserved for two hours, and that I could visit him whenever I wanted during that time slot. That's where we'll go."

"Okay," I said, and I squeezed his hand.

Eilam hugged me tight, kissed the top of my curls, and began to count down. By the count of three, we were in a narrow alleyway off Main Street in Kansas City, Missouri.

My jaw dropped. I still couldn't believe how easy he made it seem. "I'm so jealous," I said as he pulled my hand and led me to a sidewalk.

"Don't worry, we'll get you there."

It only took a few minutes before we rounded a corner and approached a building with massive books painted along its facade. It was a monster of a bookshelf.

Eilam checked the time, eyes sparkling as he said we'd have a little more than an hour to meet with him.

My anxiety peaked once we got inside and hurried around corners and down hallways. When we came to an abrupt stop, I almost tripped on Eilam's heels.

He stood in front of me and pulled a piece of debris from my hair. He didn't say anything after, he just tilted his head and smiled. That was when I realized I hadn't seen my reflection in what felt like days. I needed to look at least half decent in the presence of his freaking grandpa. "Is it me? I look crazy, huh?"

"No, you look perfect. Are you nervous?"

My eyes widened. "Yes."

He laughed. "Me too."

I shoved him a little. "What, no. You're not supposed to be nervous. *I'm* supposed to be nervous. You're supposed to be suave and cool or whatever."

He reached for my hand again. "It's just that I've never brought a girl with me before."

"Well, shit. Now I feel special."

"You are."

I tried to look away from him but couldn't. "Don't ever change," I said and I meant it. He was so great at balancing out my negativity. It was interesting how people could fit together like puzzle pieces.

We turned another corner, and there were rows of glass meeting rooms—some bigger than others. "He's in the last one," Eilam whispered, and I felt my palms get all sweaty.

When we arrived, I could see a slender Black man sitting in front of a laptop with his ankles crossed. He was dressed like someone who taught fancy literature at some expensive college somewhere.

Eilam knocked twice on the glass, and he looked up with a smile, motioning for us to come in.

His voice deep, his arms open wide. "Son, how are you?" He

smiled, wrapping Eilam into his embrace. "You've grown. I'm afraid to ask what year it is. And may I ask who this wonderful person is behind you?"

"Grandpa, this is Hylee."

"Oh, Hylee, huh? Beautiful, beautiful name. It's grand to meet you. You can call me Professor Stewart. Or just Mr. Stewart is fine, too."

I shook his hand, and he invited us to sit in the chairs across from him. "What brings you to me today, son? And with a friend!" He bounced his eyebrows up and down and winked at us. "It must be a good day. Whatever the day—can I ask what year you're coming from?"

Eilam started to say something, but his grandpa lifted a hand. "Oh no. I take that back. Please don't tell me the year. I already feel old. But the month, I'll take the month."

"It's March."

"And the day?"

"The nineteenth."

We laughed, and he nodded, pulled a toothpick from his pocket and stuck it in the side of his mouth. "What can I do you two for? It's always great seeing you, you know that. And your mom, how is she? Oh—never mind that. Go on, tell me what brings you to the library on this fine summer day? Tired of the cold?"

I smirked. I wished it were that.

"Grandpa, Hylee has a few questions about time travel. She's, uh ... she's like us."

Mr. Stewart straightened his posture. "Well, I'll be damned. Sit still, sweetheart. Let me grab my bifocals," he said, as he rummaged through a bag on the ground. He held them up to his face and peered through them until he smiled, then set them down.

"So you have the gene, huh? Welcome to the family. What are your questions?"

"Ah, yeah. I really want to know if you have any experience with time traveling to alternate dimensions?"

"Oh?"

"Yeah, I've been sucked into this dark place," I said, and I explained what the world was like there.

"I've never heard of your specific dimension, but from my research, I know it's possible. Dimensions are infinite, and they have the ability to manifest, or call out—if you will—to certain people for whatever reason. Are you, and I apologize if I'm pressing, but are you dealing with any sort of grief or loss?"

I nodded with urgency, leaning in.

He continued. "I know the darker dimensions can latch on to people like a bad omen. But did you say that the timeline couldn't be altered in this dimension you've been going to?"

"That's what it seemed like. Everything was playing out in front of me like a movie stuck on a single day."

He rubbed the beard on his chin. "Intriguing. Very, very intriguing. I can't say I have too much experience with a dimension that can't be altered by time."

"Actually, Grandpa, Hylee realized she could time travel through our current timeline, too. And, well, she—"

"I really messed up," I said, cutting in. "And I need to know how to fix it."

He folded his hands together. "Hmm, I see." We sat in silence for a couple of seconds while he adjusted his toothpick. "It *is* possible to fix it, but I need to say this before I say anything else: Altering time could be a grave and impossible task. When it's not planned, where you land could have the ability to cause a car crash—do you understand that? It takes the saying 'wrong place, wrong time' quite literally.

"With trial and error, I've found that changing the original timeline has varying effects depending on how big or how small the change. Perhaps you mend a friendship, or perhaps you do something like what you've done with Eilam today—you travel back to see me, and really you're only altering my memories, and that could change the way I make a decision, but again, that's a small change. Some might even argue that a destined change in time isn't an alteration at all—after all, can it be an altered timeline if there were never any footprints left behind?

"Here's the thing about traveling to the past. The past is fixed on a loop. When you return, you're returning to something that's already happened. When you jump into that loop, alter the way it looks, you've created a new branch. An alternate timeline, if you will. But fixing that is simple. You must return to where you altered time a few minutes before it changed, and you have to let it play out how it once did. Without you causing a ripple, the branch mends itself."

"But what happens if you have to go back repeatedly? Can something bad happen?" I felt Eilam's eyes on me when I said it.

"Of course. Bad things happen every day—with or without us altering time."

"But there are consequences, right?" Eilam said.

"Absolutely. With anything in life, there are consequences. Some of us know that better than others." He looked back at me. "Ultimately, it's up to you to decide if what you're going back for is worth altering your own future. After a while, you'll see, some things are unchangeable."

I sat back in the chair. I knew that was meant to be a warning. And yet, I didn't know if I cared. Mr. Stewart glanced at me as he adjusted his toothpick, and I think he knew exactly what I was thinking.

FORTY-TWO

When we returned to present day, Eilam drove me to Grandmommy's. He got out the car when I did, and I leaned against the passenger door.

Eilam pressed into me, and he locked a finger around one of my curls.

He kissed me, and my heart stuttered and slammed against his chest. I didn't know if I'd ever get over this forever feeling with him. Would every kiss feel like the first?

He didn't pull away after our kiss, and I locked my hands around his neck, my fingers pressing into the bumps of his spine.

I kissed him once more, and after, when we opened our eyes, his brown ones pierced mine, searching.

"I'm afraid of what might happen after this," he whispered.

"I understand. I'm afraid, too." I paused a beat. "Have you ever tried to go back in time to change the past?"

"Yes . . . and I made a lot of mistakes."

"Really? What happened?"

"When I realized I could control where I traveled to, I tried to go back in time to fix my parents' relationship. It was selfish, something I did on impulse. I had hoped that they could be back together, that our lives could be normal somehow, but it didn't work. When I returned to the present, I learned that my little brother didn't exist. . . . With my parents together again, there was no Julius."

"Oh." I tried to imagine a world without Julius's roaring laugh, and it was impossible. "How'd you fix it?"

"I had to go back, undo what I'd done. Watch it all play out and just accept it for what it was. And I realized that my parents aren't really a fit for each other anyway. I refused to see it before."

"Yeah, I can't imagine not having Julius around. He's the king of that house."

"He is . . . and also, I can't imagine this timeline without you. Which is why I'm afraid that when you walk into that house, it'll be the last time I see you, and I don't know if I'm ready for that."

"Eilam, I don't want to lose you either, but I have to do this. I have to go back. Not just for my brother, but for my dad. This is all my fault. I screwed shit up, and I have to fix it."

"But it's dangerous. Did you hear what my grandpa said back there? Any mistake you make in there could be grave."

"So what, you don't trust me? You don't think I can do it?"

"No, it's not that. I just want you to think about your plan, and how you're going to solve this. I don't want you to rush into it. You could set off the wrong outcome without even meaning to. You and I, we might not exist anymore, and you . . . you could die."

"No." My voice came out steely, determined. Eilam tried to reach for me, but I backed away from his grasp. "You can't change my mind. It's not fair for you to tell me that you've gone back to change the past and that I can't. I need to do this. This is *my* family."

"But are you hearing what I'm saying? You could die!"

I wasn't going to cry. I wasn't. But my throat tightened. I stood up straighter. "It's funny how you're such a big fan of the Avengers, but when it comes to me, when I'm the one making tough decisions, you can't even cheer me on. How pathetic."

"Come on. *Really?* So that's how you're going to spin this? Those superheroes aren't even real."

I steadied myself, feeling his words settle in me. I took a few more steps away. "But time travel is, and I have the opportunity to fix what I messed up, okay? If you can't support me, then fine, leave. I'm so sick and tired of not having someone on my side."

Eilam raised his hands, his face inflamed. "I'm not gonna sit back and watch you die. This is morbid. You can't play God, and I can't . . . I can't support this." He hurried into his car, pulled away, and didn't look back.

I waited, watched him zoom down the street, his car fading in the distance.

It felt like the darkness was crawling in my skin then, the shadows drowning my moral compass. Because it would be a lie if I said that I didn't regret the seconds I stood in the driveway, watching Eilam's car disappear.

I regretted it, but I'd made my decision, and I didn't know if I'd ever see him again.

FORTY-THREE

When I walked into the house, Grandmommy was in the living room, one of her arms crossed against her chest, the news on. The other hand holding her phone up to her ear. When she saw me, she said, "Hey, I need to call you back," and she ended the call, setting her phone on the coffee table. "Hylee, sweetie, is everything okay? Your mom and I are worried about you. How—how are you?"

I kicked off my shoes and made a sound that was a mix of anger,

"You seemed confused before you left, and if you want to talk about your dad, we can. I know we don't talk about him enough, and I'm sorry about that."

A small pin slowly fell out of Grandmommy's hair, and I couldn't stop noticing how much nicer she seemed. Was it the death of my dad that softened her? In this timeline, she'd lost both her sons, and I wanted to rush to her, fold myself in her lap, tell her how sorry I was, but I needed the truth. "Actually, Grandmommy, I'd really love to talk about Atticus. What happened to him?"

"Oh," she uttered, and she looked down at her shirt, wiped something off. I walked closer to the living room, leaned against the banister to the steps.

She cleared her throat. "When I was your age, I fell in love for the first time," she said, staring off into the distance, a small smile tugging at the corner of her lips. "And I swear, I was gonna marry that man. We met on the corner of my street—and before you go saying anything, that was normal back in my day—we were kids, hanging out in the street." She laughed softly and then stopped. "Anyway, he was in his uniform when I met him, and I'd never seen anyone like him before. My parents didn't want that, of course. But, well...I ended up pregnant, and he was sent to Vietnam." Her lips pressed thin. "He didn't return, and I gave birth to...Atticus. Eight pounds, ten ounces, and a squishy face. He was a chunk. I took him home, and we lived under my parents' roof. I was up every few hours feeding him, until one evening, he wasn't there."

My feet pressed into the floor as I stared at her. "Where did he go?"

She didn't return my stare. "I thought maybe my mother had gotten up, heard him cry, and wanted to help out, but she and my father were asleep. The windows were closed, the doors locked, and my baby was gone. When I realized, I started to panic, as anyone would in that situation, and then . . ." Grandmommy took a deep breath, her eyes focusing on her hands. "He reappeared, right in his crib, heartbeat and all. It was the strangest thing I'd ever witnessed," she said, and I covered my mouth with my hands because Atticus had disappeared and reappeared just like a glitch. Atticus and me, we could both time travel.

"Wha—"

"But the next week," Grandmommy said, cutting me off. "The next week he disappeared again, and that was the last time I saw Atticus. We searched for him everywhere, and a month later we held a funeral for him." Grandmommy turned to me, a frown on her face. "No one believed me when I told them what happened. Not my parents, not the folks in town. They said, 'That Lorraine isn't right in the head. She needs to be taken away.' And you know what I did, Hylee? I packed my things and I moved to the city. I left that life behind, and I swore I wouldn't talk about it.

"But years later, when I was pregnant with your father, there was this woman. I still don't know who she is till this day, but she came up to me one afternoon while I was grabbing groceries. She looked me dead in the eyes and she told me she *believed* me. I had no idea what she was going on about, but then she went on to say that she'd read about me in the local paper for Hill City, that she'd heard of cases like my story before. She said I held a special gene that could cause my offspring to time travel, and I didn't believe her. You know why?"

I shook my head.

"Because I believed everyone else from my hometown. I believed that I really had lost my mind. But that didn't stop me from worrying after I had your dad. I was restless, and I was so afraid that he'd disappear as Atticus had, and he never did." She sighed. "Then you were born, and one evening your dad called me, frantic. It was his first night alone with both kids, a-and he said he'd lost you. He said he only dozed off for a second, but then I heard crying on the other end of the line, and he stopped talking midsentence. He just gasped and said he had to go. It never happened again, and he never brought it up even when I asked him about it. He just said he was so tired that night, he didn't really remember what happened."

"So you *knew*?"

She gave me one nod.

"Why didn't you say anything?"

"Because I didn't know what to say, and until now, I didn't know if we'd have anything to worry about. See, you hadn't disappeared again—not until this year. I did try to do a little research, but it wasn't enough to give me answers. What you can do, Hylee..." She lowered her voice. "What you and Atticus can do, it's so rare."

So I wasn't the only one. It was me and Atticus. *Me and Atticus*, and I had so many questions, but not enough time. I gave Grandmommy a quick hug, and I rushed up the steps, ran into the room, and closed the door behind me.

FORTY-FOUR

My curls pressed into the carpet in my bedroom. One hand on my chest, the other on my stomach, as I breathed in deep and released the breath.

In and out like that until my lips felt numb.

Before I go to the dark place . . . I have to try this one thing first.

I'd wondered what would happen if I went back *further*. If I could keep Bubba from stealing the wallet . . . would it stop the break-in completely? Could everyone be safe?

I remembered the house better now, but I couldn't place where Bubba had been the day when Latrell had come over with Juice

With another deep breath, I envisioned it like I was drawing it again. The house coming into focus until I heard murmuring, people whispering sharply somewhere nearby.

Opened my eyes to find daylight hitting the white tile. I was in the first-floor bathroom, the door slightly ajar, someone out there. I stood from the tub and pulled the blinds away from the window to see what was happening outside.

Past the back porch, I could see a table set up, people laughing, my dad approaching the table with a plate in hand. Mama sipping on something in a red plastic cup. Past them, I saw a ball flying in the air. Bubba running through the gazebo to the backyard.

I'd made it to the day, but I wasn't sure if I was early or too late.

"Man, stop," someone said. The sound from the hallway coming louder, just past the door.

Another sharp whisper, and I stood. "You can't be going through my cousin's stuff. This ain't your house. Show some respect."

A man clicked his tongue, and I tiptoed to the door so I could hear better. "Stop being a little bitch. You know how much jewelry was in there? Most that shit is gold, man. You know how much we could make?" I heard him stop. "Think about it."

"Wait." And there was a pause.

"Bro, back up, don't touch me."

"Did you take any of it?"

The second voice said something I couldn't make out.

"It *is* my business. Man, please put it back. Shit. You always mess with shit that ain't yours." That was Juice. Which meant the other voice was . . .

"Shut up. You being loud." Latrell.

Something jingled. "Just put it back. Whatever you took, put it back."

He sniffed. "It's mine now. You better not say anything."

"Man, I can't take you nowhere."

"Stop being a baby."

"I'm for real."

"I'm coming back. You in, or you just gon' cry about it?"

"What do you mean you're coming back?"

"I'm pulling up. Raiding it. You see that TV in there? That Xbox? You know how much money we could get? Bro is weak anyway."

"Swear to you me you won't do it."

"Calm down. Ain't nobody gon' get hurt. I'll come when they're not here."

There was a tussle, and then I heard my mom's voice, and Juice and Latrell fled the hallway. "Yeah, yeah, I'll be right back out," she said. "Let me pee real quick."

I sucked in all the air I could. Imagined myself back on the floor at Grandmommy's house.

When I returned, I couldn't believe what I'd heard. Latrell would have broken in regardless of whether Bubba stole his wallet or not. It meant that I'd have to find another way to save Bubba and my dad.

FORTY-FIVE

PRESENT DAY: MARCH

Before I did anything else, I showered. It had been days—from what I could remember—since I'd stood on this porcelain and let the warm water wash over me, and it was so hard to make my limbs move after I turned the shower off that I slid to the shower floor, plugged the tub, and let the water fill up until my body was covered with warm water and soapsuds.

Grandmommy knocked after a while. "Hylee, you doing okay?"

"Yeah," I grunted, and she cracked the door open.

"Are you sure? I'm worried about you. Really worried. I brought tea."

I extended my hand, water dripping on the rug. "I'll take it," I said, and she walked in slowly, careful not to make a spill, even after my mess.

The moment I held it in my hands, I brought it to my lips. Lemon echinacea.

"You're so quiet in your room. You sure you don't want to go back to the city? Your mom has been asking, and I don't mind the drive."

"No thank you," I said as kindly as I could, wearing a smile.

"You sure?"

I nodded, but I wondered what my future would be if I accepted the offer. Would that mean I'd be choosing to stay in the timeline where my mom was overbearing with concern for me, and Grandmommy brought me my favorite tea while I soaked away all my worries? It would be a nice change, but I didn't know if it'd be the right change. It'd be a selfish one, and I'd chosen the selfish option many times before. I needed to do this.

"I'm sure," I promised.

As she walked away, she said, "Please be careful, Hylee." And I didn't say anything after that. I sipped my tea and sank farther into the water. I couldn't promise that.

After my hair was detangled, moisturized, and dried, I placed it in two braids. I pulled fresh clothes out of my drawers, and then I cracked the window to let the air in.

Climbed into bed, took a breath. Closed my eyes, folded my hands on my belly. Although I'd probably ruined things with him, I imagined Eilam was beside me, leaning close to whisper the steps I should be doing.

Long, fluid breaths came.

Belly up ...

Belly down ...

Rise ... and fall ...

Rise and *breathe, breathe, breathe.*

The tingling trickled to the tips of my fingers, down to my toes, and I thought of the dark place. The twisting vines, the wet thick smell of crunching, dying leaves. The way the soil covered most things. The girl, me. Eyes gone, lips a thread of silk vines. How Mama was there, in the room. How Hylee had made the bed, how the thud came. There, in that moment, I wanted to go there.

Inhaled.

One.

Exhaled.

Two.

Inhaled.

Three.

A catch, my limbs shaking. The rustling of vines on the floor, slithering around my feet. Opened my eyes, and there she was. Hylee. One step away from the door before she opened it.

That voice, out there, it called us.

She ran, and I followed. In the hall, Daddy was there, Bubba was there. He reached his hands out, wrapped himself around her as the sound of a gun went off. They disappeared. Daddy ran. Then Latrell, dressed in black, moss covering his sides, ran in the same direction as my dad.

My heart thumped, the vibration moving me forward, and with the next beat, there. There came Bubba . . . *my* Bubba.

He snapped his head in my direction, his clothes torn, a splatter of blood there, by the edge of his shirt, threads coming undone. His face was filled with exhaustion, and he took a breath. Like he wanted to fall to his knees, but he didn't.

My eyes stung, and I took a step closer.

He did, too, but his steps were more hesitant. *"Hylee?"* he said, as if I couldn't be here. As if I were imaginary. But I wondered the same about him.

In that moment, all I could do was nod, the tears slipping. It was really him, and that was his voice. That's what it sounded like. The bass in my eardrums like home. Like Mama and Daddy throwing a celebratory party because we were all home, and he wasn't a memory anymore. He was here. Alive.

I took a breath.

His shoulders eased. "You...you look so much like Mama."

Nodded again, tried to keep it together. Another step closer. Another step closer, and finally. He embraced me. My little big brother.

We hugged, the shadows perched on our shoulders. I was snot and tears, and I tensed. I'd never stayed in the dark place long enough to figure out what happened after this.

"We should go upstairs," he said, letting go and looking around. The sound of sirens came, and light bled against the walls in the darkness.

I followed him upstairs, the steps barely wooden logs, pieces of fabric clinging to them.

Bubba's room was upstairs in our old home, and in this dimension, it was similar, but the walls were worn and withered, the paint breathing with the house, the darkness engulfing most of the place.

"Have you been living here?"

He kicked away a few leaves. "If you can call it that."

My nose scrunched, trying to decipher what that meant. I paused in my steps when I heard the door open downstairs. Boots on the floor, someone on a walkie.

"They don't come up here," he said. "At least not for a while. We'll need to head to the roof. Keep out of the way."

"What happens?" I asked as he pulled back a curtain of tangled weed covering the window.

"It always grows back," he mumbled, yanking at the weeds. When they were gone, we climbed out the window, the worn shingles still rough against my palms. I followed him to where the roof hitched, looking toward the backyard.

"What did you ask?" he said, and I really had the chance to look at him now. A face like Daddy's, but years younger and older at the same time. Scars and dirt and grime. He looked like he was both fifteen and twenty-four. I wasn't sure how that worked.

"Oh." I kept staring at him. "I wanted to know what happens next. You said we couldn't stay inside."

"The police search the house for the intruders. The ambulance comes, and they take Juice's body out on a stretcher."

I tilted my head. Juice, our older cousin. He'd tried to stop Latrell from stealing, from coming back, but even if Bubba hadn't stolen the wallet, he'd have come anyway. Would it have been sooner? Or later?

Bubba kept going. "They look for me, but no one finds me. The guy gets away. The cops, the ambulance, the fire truck, they all leave. Then there's a flash of darkness and it starts over again."

"It?"

"This . . . place. Whatever it is, it begins again. It doesn't stop. I've tried changing things, but it doesn't matter. Everything gets angrier the longer it's here," he said, his knuckles scrapping into the roof. "The shadows get bigger. *They* get louder. I've watched them.... I don't know why they get upset, but it pisses me off, too." When he said that, I noticed that in the corner of his mouth, his lips stuck together a little bit. Like they were being sewn in place...

"So this place just repeats itself?"

"Yup. And every time it does, I try to find a way back home. Recently... I guess, whatever that means, I rush back to the scene in the hallway to try to wrap my arms around you, like the other me does. Every time I hope it takes me to wherever you end up, and it never does."

I was in shock now. "But wait, how did you end up here?"

He shrugged, and he touched the tear in his shirt, dried blood around it. "All I know is I was trying to protect you from getting shot, and when I grabbed you, we...we just disappeared. We glitched here for a second, but then you were gone, and I've been here since." He looked at me. "And from the way you look, I'm gonna guess I've been gone for a long time...."

Pressed my lips in, nodded my head.

"How old are you now, Lee?"

"Seventeen."

His eyes were round, brown and red-rimmed, and he stared off into the night. "So is this what it's like to have an older sister?" he asked, his voice wavering.

"I guess so."

We were silent, and below, we watched a man in black break a glass window from the garage, jump out, and run down the street. It was Latrell. It had to be.

My heart pounded as I watched him run. "Why did you do it?"

His brow furrowed at first, and then it softened as he realized. "Because we needed the money, and I heard him bragging about how he'd pawned something and got a thousand dollars in cash because of it. It didn't take much for me to grab his wallet from his pocket while he was making a plate. I just caused a distraction, and it worked."

"What do you mean we needed the money?"

"You don't remember?"

"What?" I said, almost a whisper as I tried to pull the memories together, remember the story. I remembered Daddy sold something to that white woman. I remembered I wasn't supposed to see it, and I guessed when I thought back on it—it had to be drugs. But I also remembered Bubba said Daddy had a job lined up. "You...I thought..." I fumbled. "You said Daddy had a job or something."

"It fell through, Hylee. We were broke. Daddy started dealing on the side. *Quick money*, he said. Don't you remember last

Christmas?" He paused, remembering the time that had passed. "You know, the Christmas before all this went down?"

I remembered the tree. How Bubba and I were so excited to put it up . . . but that was way before anything happened. Almost a year before. "Not really . . ."

"Daddy had his hours cut, and Mama was going to the food pantry at the church every other week. For Christmas we both got a pair of socks, a deck of cards, and a candy cane. Remember, you came home crying from school? The kids were making fun of you for wearing Walmart shoes?"

I shook my head. A memory I must have blocked out.

"I started stealing after that. Mama and Daddy thought I had a job, but I think deep down they knew what I was doing." He shrugged. "They never punished me because of it, but I guess I just stole from the wrong person."

"He would have broken in regardless. That thing you said earlier, about him pawning stuff, well, he wanted to come back anyway. Get all of our stuff."

"How do you know that?"

"Because I saw it for myself. But why—why didn't y'all tell me?"

"You were just a kid, Lee."

"So were you," I reminded.

"I'm sorry I got us in all of this. I was stupid, and I thought I was doing something."

"You were trying to help."

He lifted the side of his shirt. A wound piercing where his ribs were. It was dark, probably wet to the touch, but no blood poured out. It looked like it was frozen like that. Specks of moss covered it; small mushrooms sprouted. "I don't think I helped much."

"Does it hurt?" I asked, trying to get a better look at it from the side.

He put his shirt down. "No, but I bet it will once I make it out of here."

"But—but won't it kill you?"

"Probably."

"So then you can't leave, Bubba."

"I thought that, too, but when you're doing the same thing day after day, you really consider your options, and, Lee, this isn't a life to live. I can't keep doing this."

"But no, I can stay with you," I blurted, and I really, really could. Back home, that life, the one I'd ruined with my friends, with Eilam, it was worth leaving behind. Staying here, with Bubba, it could be easier. We could find solace, look after each other.

"What?" His voice was the sound of tires squealing on a wet street. "Did you hear what I said, Lee? The people are mad here. We can't stay. You see this stuff growing from my ribs? That ain't normal. Have you even looked at me?!"

—

I recoiled, tried to really see him through the smoky window of the moonlight again. I hadn't really noticed it before, but his face, arms—he looked skeletal. His skin stretching over milk-white bones. I think some of the wrinkles—it's what made him look older.

"We can't stay. This place ruins you. My humanity has been stripped away from me. I'm as good as dead."

"You're not dead . . . you were just gone. And you're here."

"You can't stay. *We* can't stay. I've watched them, Lee. Each time this day repeats, it feels like the house closes in on you. Like it's getting smaller. I don't want to wait anymore. I don't want to be here."

"Okay, okay. I get it. But what if—what if we can change the past? What if we change the outcome and you never end up here?"

"How is that even possible?"

"Time travel."

FORTY-SIX

PRESENT DAY: MARCH

We had a plan.

But before we could get started, I needed to tie up some loose ends.

Grandmommy was gone when I got back. I wasn't sure where— maybe she was off looking for me, but she took her car, and I needed to be somewhere.

I never got Eilam's address, but I remembered he lived by an elementary school, so I used that as the nearest landmark.

While I waited for the Uber to arrive, I tore off a piece of paper from my notepad and scribbled: *Journeys end in lovers meeting.* Folded it into fifths, shoved it in my back pocket.

The entire ride there, I chewed my lip, fiddled my thumbs. There was a good chance he wouldn't want to see me.

When I got to the school, I took off, running down the street as fast as I could, my braids slapping against my shoulders.

I swatted at bugs and ran past a few kids playing hoop. Jumped over a scooter, almost tripped, and finally, sitting in front of me, Eilam's home. Gathered all the air in my lungs before ringing the doorbell.

Some shuffling behind the door, and then the knob twisted. When it opened, Audrey stood with a smile and a mustard-yellow jumpsuit. "Hylee, it's great to see you," she said, and behind her, I heard a little kid gasp.

"Oh! Are we gonna play Smash?" Julius said.

"Bubs, Hylee is here to see Eilam, but maybe later, okay?" Audrey said, turning to him. Then she faced me again. "Come on in, he's in his room."

When I entered, I went to Julius, bending down to get to his eye level. "Next time I'm here, we'll play Smash, okay?"

His brows shot up, his jaw dropping. "Oh!"

I chuckled. "Pinkie promise," I said, and he wrapped his pinkie around mine, giggling. I ruffled my hand through his tight curls before heading down the hallway.

I waited by Eilam's door for a second. Another breath, a swallow, and then I knocked.

"Come in," I heard him say, and I opened the door slowly.

He sat at his desk, and he was turning in his chair, one earphone down. He froze for a second, and then he removed his earphones and shut his laptop. "Hey . . ." he said, but even when he said it, I could tell he wanted to know why I was here.

"Hey," I said, and I shut the door behind me.

He didn't say anything; he leaned back in his chair, hands folded in his lap, waiting.

"I'm sorry," I said, and it was all I could say at first, because I'd really messed up. I shouldn't have pushed him away like I had. He wasn't the enemy. He was a voice of reason and concern, and I just hadn't wanted to hear that.

He looked away from me.

"I know you were just being honest, and I shouldn't have attacked you. I shouldn't have spun the situation like I did, and I shouldn't have let you leave, but I needed you to know that I have to do this. I understand that it's dangerous, and that there's a high chance that I might screw shit up because I have before, but I don't want you to doubt me—not with this."

Still nothing.

"And you deserve to be pissed off. . . because I get it. By doing this, there's a chance I could erase us. And I am so scared of losing you, Eilam."

And then he sat up. "I am really afraid of losing you, too. And I shouldn't have made you doubt yourself. I know you have to do it. If I were you . . . well, you know. I'd do anything for my brother."

I bit the inside of my cheek, nodding all the while. "I know," I whispered, the fear flooding in on all sides.

He was out of his chair in a flash, rushing to me with his arms open. We embraced, pressing into each other. It felt like Eilam was the only person who understood me, and it hit hard knowing that everything could change after this. Could I live in a world with the memories of Eilam, knowing that he'd never know me the same way I knew him? And would the world be the same after the timeline was changed, once again? Would Eilam still be my Eilam, or would he be a different person entirely?

I wrapped my arm around his neck, bringing my lips to his and sticking the note into his back pocket.

"If we lose each other, and we meet again, how will we know?"

I adjusted myself in his arms, so I could see him. "I . . . I don't know. Maybe we'll just know," I said, remembering the first time I'd met Eilam. The way time felt infinite then. "Maybe it'll be a look?" I suggested.

"What? You'll just look at me, and I'll know?"

"Or you'll look at me, and I'll know you know."

"Yeah, or maybe I'll tell you."

"No, don't tell me. Don't force it. If it's meant to be, then it will be."

"I'll always want to remember you, Hylee. I can't fathom a timeline where I could forget that. You were my breath of fresh air," he said, and he kissed me like rain.

We smiled at each other after, and I never wanted to forget his smile.

I never wanted to forget him, so we kissed again and again and again, trying our best to create an infinity.

FORTY-SEVEN

The house was still empty when I got back home.

I went to my room, lay in bed, and remembered the plan. What I was hoping to pull off would take a lot of focus—and a lot of energy.

I just really hoped it worked.

With a breath, I was back at the dark place. I arrived just as the police questioned my family outside, and I snuck past the living room and upstairs to Bubba's bedroom.

Just as promised, he was waiting for me with hopeful eyes.

"Take my hand," I said, and he did. "Do you think this will work?"

He swallowed. "I hope so, Lee."

"But we have to move fast." I looked at his wound. "I just don't know how much time we'll have if we don't."

"We've got this," he promised. "It's you and me, sis. Okay?" He held his pinkie out to me, and I twisted it.

"Okay." I nodded.

We counted to three together, inhaling and exhaling. By the third breath, we left the dark place and landed on November 9, outside the house on the back porch.

We didn't have much time, but our goal was to split up. It was important for Bubba to get to the past version of himself before he got shot, and before he got stuck in the time loop I'd accidentally dropped him in.

For me, it was important that I caused enough distraction to keep my dad from being a victim, too.

Bubba climbed the side of the house, and I helped him up, hearing him wince from the pain in his side. He gave me a thumbs-up once he got the window open on the second floor, and for me, it was go time.

I peeked into my bedroom window. Inside, my younger self stood in the middle of the room, her back to me. There was a thud, and she jumped back. Any second, she'd be running for that door and to the hallway, which meant that I needed to get to the kitchen.

The storm door was unlocked, but the big wooden one wasn't. Shit. Bubba had told me it would be unlocked.

Another thud, and I was out of time. Little Hylee would be dashing for the hallway, and I had no time to break in. But I couldn't travel backward. Not without Bubba.

I tried running into the door first, my adrenaline picking up as I did it, the hit knocking the air out of my chest, but the door barely bulged. It wouldn't give.

Ran back to the window, lifted up the screen, and kicked myself through.

I flopped to the ground, and I didn't think when I landed, I just ran. Ran as fast as I could, catching the end of my name leaving my brother's lungs.

When I got to the hallway, the strangest thing happened. My brother was there, but in two forms. The version of him that belonged here, and the version of him that had been stuck in the dark place.

A shot was fired, and it pierced his side. But instead of my brother reaching out to latch on to me, the other version of him pushed both of them backward until they fell to the ground, merging into one person.

The younger version of myself disappeared without him.

I gasped, running back into my old room and hiding as I waited for the hurried footsteps to run past.

The sirens grew in the distance, and I heard glass shatter.

Ran back into the hallway to find Bubba on the ground, coughing up blood and holding his hand to his side.

My vision blurred, and no one was around when I looked. Not even Daddy. "Why did you do that?" I cried, getting to my knees and pressing my hands to his wound.

He coughed again, struggling to breathe, and I lifted his head up, so angry that he'd made this decision without me. "You were supposed to distract yourself. You weren't supposed to do this!"

His voice was broken. "I had to, Lee. Don't you see, if I wasn't there, it would have been you. You would have taken the bullet for me, and I couldn't have done that."

The tears kept coming, the sirens louder now. "No! I would have taken it for you! It was supposed to be us, remember?! It was supposed to be us!"

He shook his head. The blood pooling beneath him. "I know, I know. I'm sorry I lied, but I couldn't let you lose your life because of me."

I gripped his arm as he coughed. "No! That was stupid. This was stupid."

His eyes fluttered. He looked so tired. "I had to."

I tried to wipe his mouth so he could talk more. I didn't get enough time with him. There had to be a way to change this again.

"Just hold on," I cried. "Give me a few seconds. We can change this. Do it over."

"Don't," he said, gripping his hand on my wrist, his face turning pale. He didn't want me to go back in time to try to change it. This was final.

"But please, you're my big brother. I love you. This shouldn't have happened. It was supposed to be you and me. It was supposed to be us, like you promised."

"It's always us, Lee." His words were only bits and pieces now, and I knew I was running out of time. His gaze slipped. "Okay... You're gonna be okay," he coughed out, and I heard car doors open. It was most likely the police. Bubba said they'd be here around this time.

"Go," he said, but it was barely a breath. And I didn't want to go. I couldn't leave like this. *"Please,"* he whispered, and he held up his pinkie.

The tears came harder when I locked them together. My brother. My protector. My first best friend.

Then the voice came, someone shouting a demand. I hugged him quickly, gently set his head on the ground, and ran to my old room.

Dashed to the closet, held my arms around myself to calm down, to stop the tears.

One.

Inhale.

Two.

Exhale.

Three.

I was gone.

FORTY-EIGHT

I was surprised when I reappeared at Grandmommy's.

It was ten in the morning on Saturday, March 28. My phone was charging on the desk beside the bed, resting next to a sketch on my notepad.

A tea kettle whistled, and I stopped in the mirror to look at myself before rushing down the steps. I had on my spandex shorts and one of Bubba's old basketball shirts. My lips quivered. The tears threatened to come. No blood on me, no sign that I'd just witnessed his death.

✳

In the kitchen, Grandmommy poured steaming water into a mug. She came to a sudden stop when she saw me. "Jesus, Lee. You scared me." She checked the time. "What are you doing up so early? Are you hanging out with Sarah today?" Sarah? So I still knew Sarah. This was a good sign.

I examined the room, looking for any minute differences, but everything looked as it had before. I nodded, lying as quickly as I could. "Yeah, just wanted to see if I could borrow the car for a little while?"

She furrowed her brow, almost like she was about to say something, but she didn't. "One hour. That's it."

I exhaled, grabbing her keys. "Thanks, Grandmommy."

I turned, my braids flopping on my shoulders as Grandmommy called out to me. "And, Hylee! Please don't forget to give your parents a call. They've been asking about you."

My heart almost stopped. *Parents.* That means two. Daddy was alive. "Okay. I won't," I said, and I needed to figure out what else had changed. I pulled my shoes on quickly, tying them, and then ran upstairs to grab my phone. I needed to get to Eilam. Tell him what happened.

My hands shook as I turned the engine off and got out of the car. I rang the doorbell, shifting from side to side as I waited.

Behind the door was Audrey. Her black hair pulled out of her face. "Hi," she said, smiling, and then she snapped around. "Julius, no! Don't touch that!"

My shoulders relaxed at Julius giggling in the background, and I remembered that I'd promised him we'd play Smash.

Audrey turned back to look at me, apologizing, and before she could speak again, I said, "Is Eilam home?"

"Sorry, honey. He stayed over at a friend's house last night. I can tell him you stopped by. What's your name?"

My bottom lip trembled, and my knees grew weak. She didn't know me. "Oh—um..." My shoulders dropped. "W-will you tell him that Hylee stopped by?"

"Of course," she said, and she smiled again before she closed the door and wished me a good day.

The tears didn't wait as I rushed back to the car. I opened my phone, searching for his name, but nothing. Searched for him in my friend list on social media, nothing.

And I pressed my palms into my eyes as the tears continued to roll down. I knew he was forever gone. We were simply caught up in this time thing, and I didn't know if I'd ever get him back, if I'd ever get *us* back.

There was no reversing the damage I'd done.

FORTY-NINE

Because I needed to know, I went back in time.

Dates I scribbled on my arm in black ink. Dates I couldn't forget.

Here's what I discovered:

The day before my seventeenth birthday, I time traveled. To where? I'll never know. But it still happened in front of Lucia. She was in so much disbelief, she went looking for my parents, and moments later, they found me on the front porch, just as confused as I was.

In January, I was sent to live with Grandmommy because just

like before, my parents were afraid for me, and they didn't know what to do.

On the first day of school, I met Sarah. She still welcomed me with open arms and smothered me with her wit and fancy clothes.

I'd never made it to Kesha's party. Why? Because Lucia and I got in a fight while we were getting ready, and she left without me. Her cousins picked her up, and *I had to assume*—because I still didn't know—I had to assume that it was the last time I'd see her for a long time.

And without that party, there was no Eilam.

Six months passed. I thought about Bubba a lot, and because of that, there were a lot of tears between sketches. It seemed my drawings had always been more honest than I'd ever been, and the more I drew, the more I wanted to turn that honesty into action. But I found that my family had healed differently in this timeline now that they had definitive closure. It was still horrible and painful, but at least Bubba's disappearance wasn't a wound festering inside all of us, eating us alive from the inside out. In this new timeline, he died the night of the break-in, and while healing through that pain was horrible, we had one another.

In the spirit of my newfound honesty, I told Sarah everything

I knew about time travel. I swear, it was like a weight had lifted. She was more excited than she was afraid. She had so many questions—most importantly, could we use my ability to travel the world instead of through time? She was serious about going to New York.

I wore a stupid grin. I didn't know, but I wanted to try.

I finished junior year, and I spent the summer with my parents. They moved again; I helped them pack, and I sat them down to explain what was happening to me. I just needed to be honest. It wasn't something they fully understood, and while I wanted to tell them about Atticus, it wasn't my secret to tell.

But I did tell them that there were more people in the world like me. That I wasn't the only one. That this was genetically passed down to me.

I practiced yoga during the summer, trying my best to understand what it was like to be one with my own body, to understand the importance of breath. I thought of Eilam a lot, hearing his voice inside me say *Breathe* as I held a pose.

It wasn't perfect, and there were still days where I time traveled without meaning to, but those days came less and less often, and in August I moved back in with Grandmommy to start my senior year of high school at Lee's Summit West.

On September 16, Asia invited me to go to Kesha's party, an annual event.

Okay—*pleaded*. She pleaded, and I gave in.

I swallowed the lump in my throat as we approached the door. The same note was taped to it: PARTY IN BASEMENT.

I descended the staircase. The basement was still painted light blue, and little twinkling lights dangled from corner to corner. Boys held up the walls and the couch, and a few girls danced in the center of the room.

Asia whipped around to look at me, popping her gum. "Want a drink?"

I nodded, following her through the crowd and to the drinks table. A Red Bull was all I could manage for tonight, and Asia handed me her keys after that, stating that I'd be her and Imani's designated driver.

After a while, the room began to fill with people. More bodies on the dance floor, the temperature rising. Asia and Imani joined the crowd, and I faded to the back, finding my own wall to hold up.

Then it happened. *Eilam* happened.

I spotted him in the center of the crowd. He was speaking to someone, but he stopped when he saw me.

We locked eyes, exchanging a look, and it was almost as if time slowed as he forced his way through the people.

I felt that same feeling again, but this time, I knew him. I knew him and I remembered it all. His crooked smile in the moonlight.

The way he hugged me, lacing his arms around me. Our last kiss, the smell of coffee on his breath.

Then he was a foot away, looking at me with a knowing smile. "Hi," he said.

I'd missed his voice.

Right then, I wanted to ask him everything. Wanted to know if he'd found the note I'd left him, and if he remembered me like I remembered him.

"Hi," I said, hopeful. My smile grew as the lights glistened in his eyes, and I felt my cheeks warm. I wanted to look away, but I couldn't. I didn't want to miss any more moments with him.

He stood beside me, and for a second, I watched him watching the crowd. "Have you read *Twelfth Night* by Shakespeare?" he asked.

And I remembered my English class had gone over it last year, but most of it was a blur. Really only one thing had stuck that day. "Once," I said.

He dug his hand into his back pocket, looked at me, and slid a piece of paper into my palm. "Have we met?" he said, and I opened the note. Reading it reminded me of what his grandfather had said once, how destiny was a powerful thing.

Journeys end in lovers meeting.

ACKNOWLEDGMENTS

There are so many people I have to thank. First, I'd like to thank my husband. Thanks for loving me, supporting my art, and always venturing to the dark place with me to help me find my way out.

I'd also like to thank my family; without them, I don't know who I'd be. Big thanks to my friends who've supported me. I appreciate you. To the Lit Squad for cheering me on every step of the way and being so gracious and full of humor and hope.

As always, a world of thanks to my amazing literary agent, Katelyn Detweiler. Your enthusiasm and love for my stories are unmatched, and I appreciate you tremendously. You're the best advocate, the best business partner, and overall, just a sincerely amazing human. You're also a very talented writer. To anyone reading this, please buy her books.

Thanks to everyone else at Jill Grinberg Literary Management who have championed me. I feel so lucky to have all of you.

All of the thanks and praise to Christine Collins, an amazing editor and delightful human. I couldn't have done any of this without you. I appreciate you.

To the wonderful team at Hyperion, thank you for helping bring *The Dark Place* to the world.

Infinite thanks and gratitude to the managing editorial and copyediting team: Sara Liebling, Guy Cunningham, Sharon Krinsky, Monique Peterson, and Jody Corbett. Thanks to marketing: Matt Schweitzer, Holly Nagel, Danielle DiMartino, and Dina Sherman. Thanks to publicity: Ann Day and Crystal McCoy. Thanks to the design team for making this book so pretty to look at and easy to read: Joann Hill, Marci Senders, and Zareen Johnson. Thanks to Elena Masci for a truly beautiful and terrifying cover. Thanks to production: Marybeth Tregarthen and Anne Peters. Lastly, a big thanks to the sales team: Monique

Diman, Jess Brigman, Michael Freeman, Vicki Korlishin, Mili Nguyen, and Kim Knueppel.

And of course, special thanks to the readers, librarians, book sellers, and anyone who has helped get my words to the readers who need them. I couldn't do this without you.